"So... you can feel what I'm feeling, when I'm feeling it?"

"Yes." Brendan brushed a strand of hair away from Libra's cheek. "Although I don't always understand what I'm sensing."

Her gaze searched his, a small frown line forming between her brows. "That seems... invasive."

He winced. "I don't mean it to be. I respect your privacy. But sensing your emotions helps me understand you."

"It also gives you an advantage. You know what I'm feeling, but I don't know what you're feeling."

"Don't you?" Her fear had abated. Now it felt like she was testing the boundaries of their altered dynamic. He could help with that. "I'll bet you know what I'm feeling right now." Rather than sensing her emotions, he projected his own. All of them.

Her frown deepened for a moment, and then her cheeks flushed pink. Her breathing stuttered, too, as awareness lit her eyes. "Yes, I do."

GUARDIAN MATE

A Starhawke Sci-Fi Romance

AUDREY SHARPE

Ocean Dance Press

GUARDIAN MATE

© 2021 Audrey Sharpe

ISBN: 978-1-946759-97-9

Ocean Dance Press, LLC
PO Box 69901
Oro Valley AZ 85737

Visit the author's website at:
AudreySharpe.com

Want more interstellar adventures? Check out these other titles in the Starhawke Universe.

Starhawke Rising

The Dark of Light

The Chains of Freedom

The Honor of Deceit

The Legacy of Tomorrow

Starhawke Rogue

Arch Allies

Marked Mercenaries

Resurgent Renegades

One

Plumes of black smoke billowed out of the nose of the plane like dragon's breath.

Brendan Scott pulled the mixture back to shut down the engine and flipped off the master switch, cutting power to the electrical system.

The acrid smell of burning insulation hung in the air. He turned off the cabin heat, closed the vents, and popped open a window.

The smoke from the engine compartment partially obscured the shadowy terrain visible through the windshield. As he nudged the plane's nose toward the ground, a nearly full moon illuminated the forest of redwoods rising up to meet him.

The eerie reddish glow of flames joined the smoke. "Come on, Romeo, you can fix this." He added shallow turns to the rapid descent, darting his gaze to the air speed indicator.

Talking to the plane wouldn't help blow out the engine fire, but it worked wonders for steadying his pulse as he dove toward the trees.

The red glow flickered then vanished, the smoke stream dissipating with it.

Easing back on the yoke, he leveled off his descent, switching to problem number two—making an emergency landing in the middle of the maze of trees stretching in all directions.

He'd flown over this area of northern California dozens of times in the past twenty-five years. He knew the terrain well. However, options for landing were limited now that the fire had forced him to shut off the engine.

His gaze swept the trees, searching for the strip of solar lights that would outline the forest service road. What he wouldn't give for the heads up display his R&D department was developing for the Fleet's new Discovery-class starships. Instead he was flying with the same tech his ancestors had used more than two hundred years ago. Upgrading the vintage four-seater Skyhawk with modern equipment had seemed wrong.

He was paying for that decision now, but he wasn't without resources. Reaching to the passenger seat he snagged his night vision goggles and slid them on, which brought potential obstacles into sharp focus.

Wedging the plane in the treetops of the redwoods was a possibility, but he could be looking at a hundred-foot drop to the ground. He had safety equipment in the storage compartment, but nothing that could get him down that distance. And no guarantees on how soon emergency personnel would reach him. He could be in for a rough rescue or an untimely end if the plane slipped loose and plummeted.

The forest service road was a much better option, as long as he could locate it and reach it in time. There were no houses nearby and no power lines or other aerial traps to contend with.

He made a visual scan of the terrain, gauging the distance to the uneven surface. Still enough wiggle room to make a decent approach, assuming he was correct about the road's position. It should be to the east—

There! A glimpse of lights through an opening in the trees. The solar lamps weren't as bright as runway lights, and they were spaced farther apart along the shoulder of the road, but the nearly full moon helped illuminate the road's path. Not exactly a searchlight, but he'd located the straightest section of the road in his flightpath. A new moon would have made this a whole lot worse.

With the master switch off, he couldn't use the flaps to bleed off speed during his approach. The radio was dead, too. Thank goodness his dad had drilled him on difficult landings since he was old enough to sit in the pilot's seat. He could handle this. Visualizing his dad in the co-pilot's seat, talking him through each step, helped, too.

The trees took on distinct shapes as the plane descended toward the strip of packed earth below. He kept the nose up and the wings clear of the trees, the plane gliding down as soundlessly as an owl until the landing gear made contact and he braked, his gaze on the road ahead.

And that's when he saw movement—a shadowy shape on the road directly in front of him.

An overwhelming sense of surprise and fear swept over him as a glow bloomed like a corona a split-second before his plane impacted an invisible wall.

The force flung him against his restraints, the yoke bucking in his hands as the plane careened sideways. Another impact slammed his head against the side window in a blinding flash of pain as the sickening squeal of grinding metal filling his ears.

His vision blurred and dimmed as the plane lurched to a halt, its shuddering sigh following him down into a grey world of nothingness.

Two

Libra Hawke's heart pounded in time with her feet as she sprinted toward the downed plane, the bite of the crisp winter air creating plumes in front of her eyes.

Beams of moonlight and the road's solar lamps illuminated the tree the plane had struck. The base of the giant redwood bore ragged lacerations and bare patches of exposed bark from the collision, but the plane looked far worse. It sprawled at an awkward angle like a wounded bird. The impact had crumpled the wing on the far side, and the side facing her showed indentations on the wing and nose where the plane had ricocheted off her energy shield.

Never in a million years had she imagined a plane would drop silently from the sky onto the forest service road during her evening walk. The scrape of the landing gear on the ground had been her only warning. She'd reacted on instinct, slamming her shield up and sending the plane careening into the trees.

Had she killed the pilot and passengers?

A sick feeling gripped her abdomen as she caught a chemical smell wafting up from the ground under the plane. Leaking fuel? The plane wasn't making any sounds except for a faint metallic groan—no sign of smoke or fire.

She halted beside the passenger door, a shudder making her teeth chatter. She was supposed to protect people, not hurt them. This was her fault.

She needed Marina and Gryphon. Marina was the best hope the occupants had for survival.

Closing her eyes, she cleared her mind and sent an image of the damaged plane to Marina. *Accident! Forest road.*

Two heartbeats later, she got her response.

On our way!

Opening her eyes, she reached for the door handle. If the plane's occupants were still alive, Marina could heal them. If they weren't...

She couldn't go there. They would be fine. Had to be. And she could help. Her healing talents were weak compared to Marina's, but she could stabilize the situation until Marina and Gryphon arrived.

Bracing for what she'd find, she pulled the door open.

No one in the passenger seat. A quick check of the back seats confirmed the pilot was the only person onboard. He looked unconscious, slumped sideways against the opposite door, although his goggles hid his eyes.

He didn't move as she pulled herself onto the passenger seat, but the ambient light confirmed his chest was rising and falling with each inhalation. Not dead. Which gave her something to do.

Moving with deliberation, she eased the goggles from his face. His eyes remained closed, his breath hitching in and out, like he was in pain.

She could help with that, too.

Placing her hand on his arm, she engaged her energy field, extending it along his arm until it wrapped around his entire body. The connection made her nerve endings tingle, startling her. She glanced at his face, but his eyes were still closed.

She drove her energy deeper, blocking the pain receptors in his brain while simultaneously slowing the cellular breakdown at the points of trauma on his head and left arm.

As the energy did its work, she studied him, the moonlight casting him in shades of grey. He was younger than she'd expected, maybe a few years older than she was, his hair a similar shade of blond to hers. He was wearing a dark aviator jacket over a light-colored shirt and jeans. His restraints held him in his chair, but it looked like his head had struck the side window.

"Are you an angel?"

The mumbled words brought her gaze to his.

His eyes had opened partway. He was staring at her with a delirium-like wonder.

He was conscious. And talking. A good sign the energy was helping stabilize him. She shook her head. "No, I'm not an angel."

"Then why do you have a halo?"

Halo? She glanced up, but the only thing above her head was the low ceiling of the plane. "What halo?"

He frowned. "You're glowing."

Her heart stopped dead. Her breath, too. Then they both took off like a galloping mustang.

She knew exactly what he was talking about, but she couldn't believe it. Humans couldn't see her energy field. "You mean the moonlight?" She pointed out the windshield.

He shook his head, wincing. "No. *You're* glowing. Color and light dancing."

The mustang in her chest was joined by an elephant in her gut.

"It's beautiful." A tiny, drunken smile curved his mouth as he gazed into her eyes. "So are you."

She slammed off her energy field.

He blinked. Frowned. "It's gone."

Please, no. This couldn't be happening. There was no way he could—

"Libra?"

Marina's call made her turn. "Over here! Hurry." Because if what she suspected was true, she needed to put as much distance between herself and this stranger as possible.

Three

Brendan woke from the deepest sleep of his life with absolutely no idea where he was.

Lifting up on his elbows, he surveyed his surroundings.

The wood paneling in the bedroom gave a honey glow to the light filtering through the two rectangular windows. Redwood trees dominated the view outside, making it difficult to determine from the shadows if it was early morning or late afternoon.

The king-sized bed had soft flannel sheets in a red and green pattern of bears strolling amongst evergreen trees. The room held a faint scent of spice, maybe cinnamon and pine?

But the dominant element in the room was the plants. They filled almost every surface—perched on shelves, bookcases, and sitting in decorative pots on the floor. A small evergreen sat in one corner, its branches covered in festive red, green, and gold decorations.

Pretty and cheerful. But where the hell was he? And why couldn't he remember how he'd gotten here?

He sat up, scrubbing a hand over his face. A day's worth of beard stubble rasped on his cheeks and chin, indicating he hadn't been out for long. What *did* he remember?

He'd been on his way to San Diego in Romeo. The engine had caught fire. That he remembered clearly. He'd located the forest service road and had brought the plane in for an emergency landing. He'd touched down, hadn't he? Yes, he had. The landing gear had made contact with the road. He'd braked, but then he'd seen something on the road, followed by a flash of light. A vehicle?

An image popped into his head. A pearlescent glow, like starlight and crystal. And a woman's face, beautiful, ethereal.

His heart beat like a drum as he shoved the bedding back and moved his hands over his head, torso, and legs, testing for injuries. The left side of his head was a little tender and his left forearm showed the beginnings of a bruise, like he'd whacked it against a solid object. No indication of serious trauma, or any other bruises or bandages.

But he wasn't wearing his clothes. The navy-blue long-sleeved shirt and matching sweatpants had been turned back at the cuffs so they would fit him. The socks on his feet were his, though.

Had the plane crashed into whatever he'd seen on the road? That seemed likely considering the bumps on his head and arm and his patchy memory. But if it had, why was he wearing a stranger's clothes and lying in a stranger's bedroom? Why wasn't he at a hospital?

And what about the woman? Was she real? Or the wisp of a dream he'd conjured in his sleep?

His gaze swept the room. Someone had brought him here. Whether it was her or someone else, he needed answers.

Thankfully, he could do a little reconnaissance before coming face-to-face with whatever lay beyond the closed bedroom door.

Taking a deep breath, he calmed his mind and opened his emotional field, using the heightened empathic abilities he'd inherited from his parents to seek out other emotional resonances inside the house. He encountered only one, but it was strong. He sensed anxiety, agitation, and wariness, although nothing to suggest hostility or aggressive intent.

That was good news. And logical. Whoever had brought him here had gone to great effort to make him comfortable. They'd also let a total stranger into their home. That was bound to be unsettling. The real question was, why was he here?

Slipping out of bed, he padded over to the closed door, making as little noise as possible. He swung the door open then paused, listening. A rhythmic chopping of metal on wood came from his left. New scents greeted him as well—roasting garlic and onion.

His stomach rumbled in response.

A doorway to what looked like another bedroom sat open directly across from where he stood. A narrow hallway to the right formed the interior walls of that bedroom and what was probably the kitchen on the opposite side of the house.

He took a couple steps, surveying his surroundings.

A high counter peninsula with three bar stools separated the kitchen from the combination living room and dining room that shared a wall with the bedroom he was in.

A stone fireplace took up at least two meters of that wall, with a couch, two plush chairs, and a coffee table positioned facing it. The front door was just beyond on the adjacent wall. His jacket hung beside a longer, thicker coat on a cast iron coat tree to the right of the door. His shoes sat on a rectangular mat on the floor.

Along the wall opposite the fireplace, a dining table with four chairs stood next to a picture window looking out on a porch with a slatted railing. Judging by the view, the house was on a hillside, with the ground sloping away from the porch.

The overall effect was as cozy and inviting as the bedroom, with festive touches everywhere, the furniture worn but comfortable looking. The cabin itself had an old-world feel to it. The only sign of visible technology was a decades-old comm panel, located on the same wall as the barstool peninsula, which looked like the newest addition to the cabin's design. Pairing that info with the thicket of trees outside indicated he was still in the heart of the forest where he'd landed.

The chopping stopped, replaced by the babble of water running in the kitchen sink.

He crept toward the peninsula, peering around the edge of the wall into the kitchen.

Wow, he's tall.

He wasn't a slouch in the height department, but the man standing at the sink had him beat by half a head at least. He looked close to the same age, maybe a little older, with light brown hair cut short on the back and sides and a little longer on top. The red sweatshirt he was wearing made it hard to gauge his build, but judging by the leanness of his face, the guy was more lanky than stocky.

He glanced down at his borrowed clothes. At least now he knew who they belonged to.

"You're awake."

His head snapped up.

The man had stopped his cooking preparations and was watching Brendan with the focus of a raptor. Keen intelligence shone in his eyes. His attitude was neither friendly nor aggressive, just cautious.

"Uh, yeah." He swallowed to clear the scratchiness from his throat. "You brought me here?"

The man nodded. "You were a little out of it when we found you."

"We?"

Another nod. "My wife and I."

The woman he remembered? "Does your wife have blonde hair?"

The man's eyes narrowed, the anxiety underlying his emotional field spiking. His reply was a shade cooler. "No. Why?"

"Uh, I have this memory of a blonde woman, someone I don't know." But the way the man was looking at him now, he felt like an alien specimen under a microscope. "I must have imagined it. I'm Brendan. Brendan Scott."

"Gryphon Forrest. My wife is Marina."

Gryphon. That fit. At least this version didn't have claws and a beak. He did have an accent Brendan couldn't place, with elongated vowels and softer consonants. European, maybe? Or perhaps one of the off-planet colonies? "So, you found my plane?"

Gryphon nodded. "Heard the crash. My wife has a medical background, so she was able to determine your injuries were easily treatable."

The image of the woman's beautiful face surrounded by a halo of blonde hair and a pearlescent glow drifted into his mind again. Maybe he had seen an angel. "Guess my guardian angel was working overtime last night."

"Lucky for you."

"Yeah."

"We notified the forest service about your plane, let them know you were safe." Gryphon turned back to the array of vegetables on the counter and started chopping again, but his anxiety level didn't abate. "How do you feel?"

"My head and arm are a little sore, but not bad."

"Glad to hear it."

"What about my plane? What condition is it in?"

Gryphon flicked a glance at him. "It didn't fare so well. Collided with a tree. One wing's pretty beat up."

He flinched. Poor Romeo. In a battle with a redwood, the plane was guaranteed to lose. "Is it nearby?" Gryphon had said they'd heard the crash.

"Not far. I'll take you out there after breakfast. Marina will be back soon. Figured we should give you a solid meal before sending you off."

Sending him off. That had a finality that told him exactly where he stood. Even without his empathic senses he could tell Gryphon didn't want him here. Maybe he was a jealous husband. Or a recluse.

Gryphon picked up the cutting board and slid the vegetable slices into a large pot on the stove.

The aromas drifting on the air drew Brendan closer. "What are you making?"

"Vegetable stew."

"Smells good."

Gryphon met his gaze. "It will be." But the look in his eyes made it clear Brendan would never taste it.

He glanced down at his borrowed shirt and sweatpants. "My clothes?"

"In the dryer." Gryphon gestured in the direction of the hallway. "They got a little dirty getting you back here. Marina insisted on cleaning them."

He got the impression Gryphon had fought her on that. And lost. "Thanks for the loan."

Gryphon glanced at him and grunted.

Yeah, so not welcome here. The sooner he made tracks, the better. He just needed to locate his comband.

Striding over to the coat tree, he stuck his hand in the pockets of his jacket but came up empty. "Where's my comband?"

"You mean this?" Gryphon held up a strip of interwoven fabric and metal.

Even from across the room he could tell the comband wasn't in good shape. He crossed back to Gryphon. "What happened to it?"

Gryphon handed over the mangled forearm sleeve. "Looked like you smacked it against the door during the crash."

Brendan examined the comband. The surface display had cracked open in a starburst pattern consistent with severe blunt trauma. But a force that strong should have shattered his arm at the same time.

He flexed the fingers of his left hand, feeling the slight twinge along his forearm where the comband normally rested. Either he'd gotten incredibly lucky and the comband had absorbed the blow perfectly, or Gryphon wasn't giving him the full story.

His empathic senses were leaning toward option two, which gave him added motivation to get the hell out of here. "Can I use your comm panel's direct line?"

Plucking a towel from the hook beside the sink, Gryphon dried his hands. "If you don't mind the lack of privacy."

The not-subtle mocking in that last statement cleared away any hesitation he might have had. "No problem."

Moving to the panel, he inspected the unit. Yep, old tech. Barebones, too. Audio only, and no vid camera. He could feel Gryphon's gaze on him as he called up his personal account and contacted his P.A.

Mary Kay answered immediately. "Where are you?" Her voice was pitched higher than normal, tension evident in every syllable. "I got a call from the forest service late last night that your plane had gone down but you were okay. When you didn't call—"

He winced. "Sorry to worry you. I just now got to a comm."

"*Are* you okay?"

"Yeah, I'm fine." Although he had a growing number of unanswered questions about how exactly he'd ended up here.

A pause. "You don't sound fine."

She knew him well. Mary Kay had been his parents' P.A. since he was in diapers. She didn't have any kids of her own, so he'd been the recipient of all her motherly affection and concern.

But he was acutely aware of his audience. He glanced at Gryphon, who was watching him without making any effort to hide his eavesdropping. "It's a long story, and I still don't have all the info. Romeo's pretty banged up. I'm going to go check on him in a little bit. I'll know more after that."

"Do you want me to send out the crew? They're on standby."

"Not yet. I'll contact you a little later after I've assessed the situation." Although without his comband, he'd have to rely on Gryphon's generosity.

"If you're sure."

He barely contained a grimace. *Not at all.* "I am. And thanks. I'll talk to you soon."

He closed the connection and glanced at Gryphon, who was stirring the stew pot but still staring at him.

"Girlfriend?" Gryphon asked.

He snorted. "My sixty-four-year-old P.A." He enjoyed the look of surprise on Gryphon's face. But it quickly switched back to wariness.

"Your clothes are probably done by now. I'll go check." He rounded the counter peninsula, brushing past Brendan as he headed down the hallway.

Brendan blew out a breath. He wasn't used to such open antipathy, especially directed at him. Most people liked him from the get-go. His empathic abilities allowed him to read their emotions and put them at ease.

Which made Gryphon's reaction even more bizarre. It wasn't like he'd tried to crash his plane in this man's backyard, disrupting his life. He'd much rather be in San Diego right now, preparing for the air show, not stuck in a forest cabin with a surly host. This detour wasn't part of his plan, either.

Gryphon reappeared in the living room, carrying Brendan's long-sleeved shirt and jeans draped over his arm. "Here you go." He thrust the clothes out. "You can leave what you're wearing on the bed."

"Okay." He paused halfway to the bedroom. Now that he was moving around, nature had made an urgent request of her own. "Uh, where's the bathroom?"

Gryphon gave him a sideways glance, his lips thinning. "End of the hall."

Oh, yeah. The sooner he got out of here the better.

Four

The creak and thump of the front door opening and closing, followed by a woman's voice and a child's high-pitched laughter reached him through the closed bathroom door as he changed into his clothes, still warm from the dryer.

He paused, listening, but whatever was being said was too muffled to understand. However, he could pick up on the emotional state of the new arrivals. Their energetic, joyful emotional fields stood in marked contrast to Gryphon's wariness and hostility.

Quickly pulling his shirt over his head and running a hand through his hair to tame the natural wave, he headed out the door, making a quick detour to place his borrowed clothes in the laundry room.

A little girl of three or four skipped down the hallway toward him, her dark hair held back from her face by a headband. She stopped, staring at him with wide brown eyes. "Hi."

He crouched, bringing himself to eye level. "Hi, yourself. What's your name?"

"Lelindia."

He smiled at the slow, steady way she said it, like it was a new skill she'd just mastered and wanted to show off. She had a slight accent, too, though not as strong as Gryphon's. "Nice to meet you, Lelindia. I'm Brendan."

Her adorable face scrunched up as she considered him. He must have passed muster, because she broke into a smile and bounced on her toes. "Wanna see my room?"

"Uh, sur–" He broke off as a dark-haired woman moved into the hallway.

She was an older version of the little imp in front of him, with the same dark hair and brown eyes but a more angular look to her features. Unlike Gryphon, she didn't give him the stink eye. In fact, she smiled as she gazed at the two of them. "Not right now, firefly. I need to talk to our guest."

"Okay, Mommy." Lelindia smiled and waved as she skipped past him. "Bye."

"Bye." He watched her until she rounded the corner. Quite a kid. Hard to believe she was related to Gryphon.

Facing her mother, he stood. "I'm Brendan."

"I'm Marina. It's good to see you up and around."

Her accent matched Gryphon's, but he still couldn't place it. "I understand I have you to thank for taking care of me."

Her soft smile returned. "You're feeling all right?"

Totally different reaction than Gryphon. He could feel her concern for his wellbeing. "A little sore, but otherwise okay."

"That's good."

He glanced in the direction of the kitchen, where he could hear pots and pans banging. "I hope it wasn't an imposition."

Her emotional field wavered, her gaze following his toward the kitchen. "Not at all. We're happy to help."

Uh-huh. *She* might be, but he knew for a fact Gryphon wanted him gone yesterday.

She motioned him forward. "While Gryphon's fixing breakfast, let's talk on the deck. It's a lovely morning."

"Um, sure." He could imagine how Gryphon would feel about that, but he also got the distinct impression Marina was calling the shots in this situation. He'd be wise to follow her lead.

She waited in the living room while he put on his shoes and jacket, then led him to the side door, passing through the kitchen on the way. Gryphon stood at the counter, a scowl on his face as he cracked eggs into a bowl.

Brendan bit back a smile. He had no doubt Gryphon was thinking of him as he beat the eggs into submission.

The tangy scents of the forest surrounded him as he stepped onto the deck, the call of the birds and whisper of the breeze carrying away the tension that had been building while he'd been dealing with Gryphon.

Marina sat in one of the four wooden deck chairs. He settled into one beside her with a sigh.

"Lovely, isn't it?" She gazed at the trees with reverence.

"Yes, it is."

"I can lose hours walking through these woods." Her focus shifted to him. "Are you from this area?"

"Uh, no." But tuning into her emotional state made him appreciate his surroundings even more. "I was on my way to San Diego when my plane's engine caught fire."

She nodded, like that was a completely normal experience. "Is that your home? San Diego?"

Interesting. Most people would have zeroed in on the dramatic fire aspect of his answer, not his destination. "Not exactly." He didn't want to go into the long version of his family history, so he went with his standard answer. "I travel a lot, so I call quite a few places home."

Some of the light went out of her emotional field. "I see."

He sure didn't. He felt like he'd blown a critical question on a test he hadn't even known he'd been taking. "What about you? How long have you lived here?"

Another flicker in her emotional field, this one of unease, although her expression remained unchanged. "We've been here almost nine years. It feels like home. And Lelindia was born here."

So he was right, they weren't native to this area. Mention of the little girl made him smile. "She's adorable."

Marina smiled, too. "Yes, she is." Her gaze moved off into the forest. "And growing up fast." A new emotion flowed from her, a yearning of some kind.

He couldn't shake the feeling she wanted something from him, but for the life of him, he couldn't imagine what it could be.

Picking a focal point on a nearby tree, he concentrated on his empathic senses, working to pick up any nuances that might help him solve the riddle. The eagerness he'd sensed from her before was still there, but much more subdued. A sadness had joined it, but it didn't feel like her sadness, more like empathy for someone else's pain.

But whose? Not her daughter, surely. That bright light didn't seem to have a care in the world. No wonder her mother had nicknamed her firefly. And while Gryphon definitely had issues, his antagonism felt temporary, a result of his current circumstances rather than a perpetual state.

Maybe he was trying too—

And that's when he felt it. A new source of emotional resonance—anxiety, curiosity, longing, and sadness. The kind of sadness that resulted from deep emotional trauma.

If he hadn't opened his empathic senses fully, he may not have picked up on it. But now that he had, it shone like a star. And it was close.

Someone was watching him.

Five

Libra pressed her back against the tree trunk, her heart going like a woodpecker in her chest. Gryphon had recommended she stay in the greenhouse until the stranger was gone, insisting that it wasn't safe for her to see him again, not after she'd told them what the man had said about her energy field.

He'd seen it. But how? How could he possibly see it? Humans couldn't see Suulh energy fields. She'd learned that fact years ago while they'd been living on Gaia, and it had held true with every Human they'd encountered since arriving on Earth.

Except him. This mysterious man who'd dropped out of the sky and blasted her quiet life into pieces.

Marina had disagreed with Gryphon's assessment. She'd been intrigued by the idea that the stranger could see Libra's energy field and had encouraging her to stay in the cabin.

She hadn't been intrigued. She'd been terrified, and her fear had made her side with Gryphon.

So she'd fled to the greenhouse at first light. It was the right thing to do. The wise thing to do. But as soon as she'd sensed the stranger moving around the cabin, she hadn't been able to keep still.

And that was another point that threw her off balance. She could sense him, as clearly as she sensed Marina, Gryphon, and

Lelindia. Which was impossible. He wasn't Suulh. He was Human. She shouldn't have been able to know when he'd gotten out of her bed. Or walked to the kitchen. Or down the hallway.

But she had, tracking every movement, each change tugging at her, urging her closer.

She'd left the greenhouse in frustration, planning to take a walk through the woods that would put more distance between them. Instead, her feet had directed her toward the cabin.

Which was why she'd been pressed up against a tree to the right of the deck when Marina had walked outside with the stranger. The scrape of wood on wood had told her they'd sat down, their voices a murmur on the breeze.

Her anxiety sat like a chill under her skin that had nothing to do with the outside temperature. But it was losing ground to the warmth flowing through her veins as the man's voice drifted to her. She couldn't make out his words, but the rich tones brought back the memories of the previous night.

When he'd called her an angel. And said she was beautiful.

She wasn't used to strangers telling her she was beautiful. She'd always maintained a certain emotional distance from the locals in town, keeping anyone who took an interest in her at arm's length.

But she couldn't seem to keep her distance from this stranger. She wanted to know more about him before he vanished from her world as quickly as he'd appeared.

The voices from the deck went silent. He hadn't moved. She could pinpoint which chair he was in without even looking. What were they doing?

Peering around the tree trunk, she got a profile view of him as he gazed at the trees. He looked even more appealing in the sunlight.

And then his gaze swung in her direction.

She snapped back around the tree, the woodpecker in her chest flying up into her throat. Had he seen her?

A creak of wood, and footsteps. His footsteps. He'd moved to the edge of the deck.

"Hello?"

Her fingers fisted, her back pressing so tightly against the tree she could have melded with it. But was she hiding? Or fighting the urge to show herself?

"Is someone there?"

Oh, stars. She had about two seconds to decide between playing statue or facing the man who had drawn her here.

The magnetic pull he exerted won out.

Taking a deep breath, she stepped around the tree. A jolt went through her body as her gaze locked with his.

His eyes widened and his lips parted in surprise, his hands gripping the deck railing. "It's you."

One question answered. He remembered her.

"My guardian angel."

Second question answered. He remembered seeing her energy field, too.

A tremor passed over her, but whether from anxiety or eagerness, she couldn't say.

He stared at her without blinking, the look on his face indicating he expected her to disappear in a puff of smoke.

She took a few tentative steps toward the deck. "I'm not an angel."

He finally blinked, coming out of his semi-trance. "You look like one."

He stated it so matter-of-factly that she glanced down, afraid she'd engaged her energy field without realizing it. No. But the drape of her white coat did have an angelic robe look to it.

She met his gaze, another zing of awareness shooting through her. "Definitely not an angel."

He moved toward the steps, his gaze never leaving hers. "Who are you?"

"My name is Libra." Or at least it had been for the past thirteen years.

"Hello, Libra."

An invisible cord drew her across the leaf-strewn ground as he descended the steps. "What's your name?"

He halted as they came within touching distance. "Brendan."

"Hello, Brendan." She tested his name on her tongue, enjoying the texture of it. Pronounced a little differently, it could almost be a Suulh name.

Seeing him in this light had a powerful effect on her breathing. His eyes were a shade of blue that reminded her of the early morning sky. Arresting eyes. He seemed to be looking right into her soul.

"I thought I'd imagined you."

"You didn't."

He lifted a hand as if to touch her, but let it fall. The smile that curved his lips made her stomach flip. "So I see."

She was seeing, too, drinking in the sight of him in huge gulps. Last night she'd felt a tug of attraction when he'd spoken to her, and again while she'd watched Marina and Gryphon settle him into her bed. But that was nothing compared to the emotions his nearness and easy smile were generating now.

The side door opened behind him, drawing her attention. Gryphon stepped onto the deck. A threatening scowl darkened his face as he spotted her and Brendan. His gaze moved to Marina, who stood at the railing, watching them. "Can I talk to you for a moment?"

She shot Libra a look that clearly said she'd handle the situation. "I'll be back."

As the door closed behind them, Brendan turned to her, his voice low. "He doesn't like me."

She shook her head. "It's not personal. He's cautious. We've never had anyone at the house before."

"Oh." He glanced at the door, then back at her. "How exactly did I get here? I remember landing the plane, but the rest is fuzzy."

"Really?" She frowned, feigning confusion. But she knew exactly why he had no memory. Marina had sedated him as soon as she and Gryphon had arrived on the scene. He'd been unconscious for the healing session in the plane, the long debate that had followed, and the slow trek back to the cabin. "You were talking when we found you."

That much was completely true. He'd suffered a serious concussion and fractured forearm, but thanks to Marina's healing touch, a medical scan wouldn't reveal any sign of prior trauma now.

After Marina had stabilized him, allowing just enough soreness and tissue damage to remain to allay suspicion, Gryphon had been in favor of leaving him in the plane for the emergency crews to find. But Libra had nixed that idea, despite the fear his comments had triggered. She'd been responsible for his injuries, and the damage to his plane. She couldn't abandon him without making sure he was okay. Which is why they'd used the collapsible stretcher to get him here. And why she'd insisted on putting him in her bedroom.

"We talked? What did I say?"

Anxiety pricked her neck. How to answer? She didn't want to repeat what he'd said about her energy field and stir up latent memories. "Um, you asked if I was an angel." He'd already mentioned that after he'd spotted her behind the tree. She gestured at her white coat. "I was wearing this last night, too."

He studied her, the feeling that he was looking into her soul intensifying. "I slept in your bedroom, didn't I?"

She nodded. It was the least she could do after nearly killing him with her shield. "You needed a place to rest." But gazing into his eyes while picturing him lying in her bed wasn't making her feel restful.

The focused intensity in those blue depths melted to something warmer. "And I slept very well, thank you. But I hate to have put you out."

"Lelindia didn't mind sharing with me." And considering how aware she'd been of Brendan's presence in her bedroom, it was a wonder she'd gotten any sleep at all.

"I met her, too." He smiled. "We got along fine."

"I'll bet." Lelindia viewed everyone as a potential friend, which was one of the things Libra loved most about her.

"Is she your niece?"

Back to choppy waters. Providing him with more information was a bad idea, so she gave him the standard response she used when anyone noted their unusual blended family. "In a way. Marina and I grew up like sisters." Usually that answer kept people from asking pointed follow-up questions.

"What about your family? Where are they?"

Clearly Brendan wasn't like most people. "They're dead." The blunt delivery was followed by the familiar stab of pain and grief that always struck on the rare occasions she allowed herself to think of them.

He startled her by clasping her hands in his, sending shockwaves along her nerve endings. "I'm sorry." His thumbs stroked over her fingers, the gentle caress acting like a soothing balm to her emotional flareup. "My parents died a couple years ago. I know how painful that loss is."

He'd lost his parents, too? She hadn't expected that, but she saw a reflection of her own grief in his eyes, and an understanding that loosened her tongue. "They died when I was eight. Marina and Gryphon have looked after me ever since."

"Really?" His eyes widened. "They don't seem that much older than you."

"Almost ten years."

"Huh. Which made them eighteen when they took you in?"

"Roughly." Gryphon had done the math to convert Feylahn years into Earth years to approximate their ages.

"That's a huge responsibility." He looked over his shoulder at the closed door. "I can understand why they'd be protective of you."

Protective wasn't quite the right word, but she wasn't about to explain the nuance of their relationship. Or that, despite their age differences, she was the leader of their family unit.

Brendan turned back, his gaze meeting hers. "There's more to it than that, isn't there? More than overprotective behavior?"

He was way more perceptive than any Human she'd met, something she should have anticipated after he'd seen her energy field. She'd need to tread carefully. "It's complicated."

A hint of his smile resurfaced. "That I believe. But I'd like to learn more." He gave her hand a light tug. "Will you come sit with me?"

She hesitated. Warning signs flashed from her logical mind, but a more elemental part of her yearned to explore this new and strange connection, to find out where it led. Talking to him, touching him, felt natural, right. Why? What was it about him that affected her so strongly?

Only one way to find out. "I'd like that very much."

Six

His angel was real. Flesh and blood, breathtakingly beautiful, and drawing him like a magnet.

Her blonde hair fell like a silk curtain around her shoulders, emphasizing the otherworldly image he couldn't get out of his head. He kept a firm grip on her hand as they climbed the steps and crossed the deck to the chairs.

Finding out she was an orphan made her hesitancy more understandable. She'd lost her parents at a much younger age than he had, and he knew how that could change a person. He'd processed much of the pain from his parents' deaths, but it still snuck up on him at odd moments, like a broken bone that had knit together but still ached. Her grief was tangible, a wound that had never fully healed even after all these years.

Her pain called to his empathic senses, affecting his reactions. He'd never been this open with a woman before, certainly not at the beginning of... whatever this was. Experience had taught him that most people couldn't handle the emotional honesty he felt. But from the moment he'd sensed her presence, he'd connected with her on a fundamental level, and her emotional responses to their interactions had solidified that impression.

Not that she didn't have secrets. Her comment about complications rang true. She knew a lot more than she was sharing. And her emotions continued to shift like liquid mercury. But the anxiety he'd sensed had faded, replaced by the stirrings of emotions that made his mind and body sit up and take notice.

He didn't need his empathic senses to figure out she was attracted to him. The warmth in her blue-grey eyes and the flush on her pale skin made that clear. Touching her created a fascinating dichotomy, both calming and exciting him at the same time. He sensed the same reaction in her.

Claiming the chair to her left, he scooted it closer and sat with his elbows on his thighs, so their knees almost touched. He didn't let go of her hand, either. "You fascinate me."

Her eyes widened, but her emotions spoke of curiosity, not fear. "Do you always say what you're thinking?"

He smiled. "As opposed to what I think people want to hear?"

She nodded.

"No. But I can't seem to help myself with you."

"Why?"

"I don't know." Her accent captivated him. He could listen to her all day. The rest of her appealed to him, too. He tilted his head, allowing his gaze to rove over her face, noting the graceful curve of her cheekbones, the curl of her dark lashes, her plump lips. "You're different. Something about you is just... different."

Her anxiety bubbled back to the surface.

"Which is a good thing," he hastened to add. "I like different." He'd spent his entire life exploring different star systems, different planets. He'd met members of the Kraed race, the first alien species humans had encountered, the race responsible for helping his ancestors develop interstellar technology.

One day, he hoped to encounter another new species, maybe one who would want to join the Galactic Council. But right now, he was much happier being at this rustic cabin in the woods with his mysterious angel.

She gazed at him through her lashes. "You're different, too."

"What makes you say that?" She was right, of course, but he wanted to hear her observations.

"You knew I was behind the tree, didn't you?"

He wasn't the only one saying what he was thinking. "I knew you were nearby, but not exactly where."

Her fingers tightened on his in an unconscious gesture as curiosity and anxiety twined in her emotional field. "How?"

"I'm an—"

The creak of the door was followed by a very loud throat clearing. Gryphon's.

He released his hold on Libra's hand and looked up.

Gryphon's eyes still held a note of warning, but his emotional field wasn't as antagonistic as it had been earlier.

Marina must have gone to bat for him.

"Breakfast is about ready. Libra, why don't you go help Marina. I want to talk to Brendan for a moment."

Libra frowned, a flicker of annoyance in her emotional field as she stood. "All right." She glanced at Brendan as she passed Gryphon, murmuring something that sounded like *be civil* as she stepped into the house.

Brendan stood as well.

Gryphon closed the door behind Libra, leaving them alone on the deck. He looked like a soldier guarding the castle gate. "Marina seems to think Libra's taken a liking to you."

"Yes, she has. I like her, too." Though *like* didn't accurately describe the emotions she'd inspired. Or what he'd felt coming from her. He'd never been so tuned into another person in his life, and he wanted to find out why.

"You're awfully sure of yourself."

He sensed both censure and respect from Gryphon. "I don't want any misunderstandings."

Gryphon folded his arms over his chest. "Neither do I. So, let me make one thing perfectly clear."

He half expected Gryphon to pull a shotgun from behind his back. "Okay."

"That girl is special."

No argument there, although Libra certainly wasn't a girl anymore, no matter how Gryphon might view her.

"She's been to hell and back, suffered more sorrow than any person deserves in a lifetime. More than you can possibly imagine."

His chest tightened. Gryphon was confirming what Libra had already told him about her parents, but it sounded far worse coming from him. What exactly had happened to them?

"She's made it through without letting it break her. She's stronger than she looks."

He believed that, too. Underneath her anxiety, he sensed a foundation of pure steel.

"Which is why I'm not about to let some rich, hotshot flyboy take advantage of her good nature and cause her additional pain."

The condemnation cut deeper than it should have. "Is that what you think I am?"

"That's what I know you are. You were flying an antique plane solo at night over rugged terrain—a reckless choice—and were forced to put it down on the forest road after the engine caught fire. That took guts, I'll give you that, but that plane didn't come cheap. Neither did that fancy communication band of yours. And now you're trying to charm the first pretty girl you see—"

"You're wrong." He held onto his temper, keeping his voice level. "Yes, I have money, and yes, I chose to make a nighttime solo flight. But I've logged more hours in the air than you can possibly imagine. There was nothing reckless about it. And I'm not trying to charm Libra. I feel a connection to her. I don't know why, but I'd like a chance to find out. Clearly, you don't want to give me that chance. Or any chance."

Gryphon's eyes narrowed, making him look more like his namesake. "So you admit you have money?"

He shrugged. "It's not a secret. Is that a crime in your world?"

"It's not a mark in your favor." Gryphon's stance shifted, his tall frame completely blocking the door. "If you want back in this house, you need to give me one solid reason why I should let you anywhere near Libra."

He wasn't entirely convinced Gryphon held that power in the household. But he didn't want him as his adversary, either. That wouldn't help his cause. What reason could he give that Gryphon would accept? "Because Libra wants me here. And she's a very insightful, intelligent woman."

Gryphon's lips pursed. "You've got that right." He stared at Brendan for several seconds, assessing. Or reassessing, perhaps, as the belligerence slowly faded from his emotional field. He sighed, nodding toward the door. "Come on. Might as well get you fed."

Brendan didn't move. "And on my way?"

Gryphon gave a reluctant shrug. "That'll be up to Libra."

That was an answer he could live with. "Fair enough." He stepped forward. "Lead the way."

Marina stood in front of the stove, transferring a pan of scrambled eggs into a serving bowl. Libra was next to her, pulling plates and bowls out of the cupboard while Lelindia bounded between them. Libra glanced at him with a worried frown.

He smiled, wanting to chase the frown away.

She looked at Gryphon as he moved to the sink, then back at him, her own smile coming out from behind the clouds.

The effect lit him up like sunshine.

"Ready to eat?" she asked.

"Absolutely. How can I help?"

She held out five large plates to him, then handed five bowls to Lelindia. "Can you please show Brendan how to set the table?"

The little girl nodded vigorously but took the bowls with care. Walking like she was on a tightrope, she wove a path to the table, the bowls clutched tightly in her hands. He followed behind, working to hold back a smile as he admired her earnest attention to her task.

She set the bowls on the oval table's short end before turning to him. "Plates go here." She tapped the center of the woven placemat to her right. He set down one of the plates as she lifted one of the bowls from the stack. "Bowls go here." She put it down in the upper left corner next to the plate.

"Got it."

She lifted her slightly smaller stack and moved to the next place setting on one of the table's long sides. He put down a plate, then she put down a bowl. She checked his work before nodding and moving on.

Cutest kid he'd ever met. And very well mannered. Marina and Gryphon were doing something right. Then again, they'd filled the parental role for Libra when they'd still been teenagers themselves. That took a leap of faith. And a hell of a lot of dedication. He'd be wise to remember that.

By the time he and Lelindia had finished adding silverware to the table arrangement, Gryphon was finishing up a fresh fruit salad and Marina had carried over the platters of eggs and roasted potatoes. Libra placed large steaming mugs of tea at four of the place settings and a half-sized mug by the chair Lelindia had just climbed onto. "You'll be sitting beside Lelindia," she murmured, "at her request."

He looked down at the little girl, who was beaming at him. "I'm honored."

He waited until Libra claimed the chair to his right before sitting down beside his new best friend.

"I love breakfast!" she announced, digging in as soon as her parents had joined them and dished up her plate.

"So do I," he agreed, popping a forkful of potatoes into his mouth. And paused, savoring the flavors that made his taste buds sing. He glanced across the table at Gryphon. "These are *really* good. Maybe the best I've ever tasted."

Gryphon's brows lifted, the barest hint of a smile softening his mouth. "That's quite a compliment." *Coming from a rich man* the look in his eyes added silently.

"I mean it." He tried the eggs next, which had mushrooms, peppers, spinach, and herbs mixed in. The flavors rivaled meals he'd eaten at the finest restaurants in the world. Or offworld. He gazed at Gryphon with new respect. "This is amazing. Where did you train?"

"Train?"

"To be a chef."

Gryphon shook his head. "No formal training. Just family recipes. And a love of edible plants."

Wow. If he wasn't absolutely certain Gryphon would reject the idea, he'd offer him a job. His personal chef was good, but if this meal was any indication, Gryphon could run rings around him.

"What about you, Brendan?" For the first time Gryphon looked at him with amusement rather than suspicion. "What do you do when you're not flying?"

It could have been a shot across the bow question, but it didn't have that feel. Gryphon seemed genuinely curious. "I work in the aerospace industry."

Libra stiffened, a tremor of alarm passing through her emotional field.

Odd reaction.

Or maybe not. If her parents had died in a plane crash or starship accident, that could give her a strongly negative association with aerospace.

Unfortunately, that would suck for him.

Gryphon, on the other hand, engaged fully. "Planes or spacecraft?"

"Both. Everything from two-passenger planes to Fleet starships."

"Really? What's your job?"

Libra wasn't looking at him anymore, her gaze on her plate as she picked at her food. Anxiety and sadness had pushed to the front of her emotional field.

He couldn't believe Gryphon would be acting so cavalier if her parents had died in a crash. Which meant there was another reason this topic bothered her. He'd have to tread lightly until he figured out what it was. "I'm a supervisor." *Of the entire company.*

"That's why you travel a lot?" Marina asked. "For work?"

"Mostly, although as a pilot, I take trips for fun, too."

But the person not having fun right now was Libra. Her pained melancholy settled over him like a wet blanket. He needed to change the subject, fast.

He gave her knee a nudge with his. "I was really impressed with the plants in your room. Do you care for them all yourself?"

She lifted her head, meeting his gaze. "Yes."

He hated the dullness that had crept into her eyes, but a small spark glowed in their depths. He wanted to fan that flame. "They're lovely."

"That's nothing," Marina said, her gaze shifting briefly to Libra before returning to him. She'd noticed the emotional downturn as well. "You should see the greenhouse."

"You have a greenhouse?"

Marina nodded. "It was a necessity. Five years ago this cabin looked like an arboretum. You could barely walk through it. That's when we got permission to convert the old storage shed into a greenhouse, so Libra and I could indulge our love of plants without having them take over the cabin. We grow our own food."

That helped explain why Gryphon's meal tasted so amazing. Everything was fresh from the greenhouse.

"Do you ever sell what you produce?" he asked Libra.

She nodded, joy returning to her blue eyes. "We have a stall at the farmers market on the weekends. We sell whatever we can't eat, and whichever cuttings are doing well."

After seeing her bedroom, he couldn't imagine any plant not thriving under her care. "Have you ever thought about expanding? Opening your own plant nursery?" Because he would finance it right now if she was interested. No strings attached.

She pulled back, like he'd startled her. "No."

"Why not? Clearly you have the talent."

She glanced at Marina, her emotions swinging back toward agitation. "I don't know. That's not something... well, it would be complicated."

There was that word again. Complicated. For a woman living a very simple life, she certainly had a lot of complications. But pushing her wasn't a good idea. Not everyone had the lofty goals he did.

He shrugged, backing off. "Just a thought. Would you show me the greenhouse?"

"Um, okay." Her breathing changed, a flush rising to her cheeks. "I could take you after breakfast."

Gryphon made a low noise, but when Brendan looked at him, he was staring at his plate.

Talk about skating on razor-thin ice with no idea when he'd fall through. Not a sensation he was used to, given his empathic advantage.

"I want to go, too!" Lelindia gave him a big smile before spearing a potato chunk and popping it into her mouth.

He returned her smile. "Okay with me, if it's okay with Libra."

The little girl's enthusiasm brought a smile to Libra's lips as well. "Of course. Those herb seedlings are due for a transplant. You can help me get them settled in new pots."

Lelindia practically bounced out of her chair. "Oh, goody!"

Libra met his gaze, amusement dancing in her eyes. "She likes plants, too. Especially herbs."

"I gathered that." He held her gaze, warmth spreading out from his chest as he basked in the glow from her eyes.

Her cheeks tinged a darker shade of pink, but she didn't look away.

"Eat up, then," Gryphon said, much louder than necessary. "And maybe after the greenhouse visit, Brendan and I can go take a look at that plane."

Right, the plane. He'd been so focused on Libra he'd bumped Romeo completely out of his mind. He needed to evaluate the situation so he could give Mary Kay instructions. And the walk would give him an opportunity to ask Gryphon some important questions about Libra.

He met Gryphon's gaze and nodded. "It's a plan."

Seven

Libra hadn't felt so topside-down since she was eight. Minute to minute her emotions flip-flopped, making it impossible to get her bearings.

Only Brendan seemed solid, his presence shining like the north star as they strolled down the dirt path to the greenhouse. Lelindia skipped ahead, calling out greetings to the birds and squirrels in the nearby trees.

"I'm sorry I upset you."

She glanced at him. The dappled sunlight on his blond hair made it shine like a halo. Maybe *he* was the angel, not her. He had fallen from the sky. "You didn't."

He gave her a look that was both firm and gentle. "I thought we were being honest with each other."

She looked away, flustered. Being honest about her thoughts and feelings was one thing. Being honest about her past was something else entirely. She needed a way to explain without betraying her secrets. "I had a bad experience with flying when I was a child."

He was silent for a moment, the dirt crunching under their feet. "Is that how your parents died? In an accident?"

"What? No, they didn't." Although that would have been far kinder. "I just... don't like to fly."

He nodded, understanding and compassion in his eyes. "I get that. A lot of people are afraid of flying, especially if they've had a traumatic experience they never processed." He touched her hand, brushing his fingers lightly over hers, sending tingles dancing up her arm. His touch grew stronger as he clasped her hand in his sure grip. "I might be able to help you overcome that fear."

Fear wasn't the dominant emotion on her mind right now. In fact, she couldn't label what she was feeling, other than warm. "I don't think so."

He squeezed her hand. "Don't be so sure. Helping people process emotions is one of my fortes."

"What does processing emotions have to do with aerospace?"

He smiled, drawing her attention to his mouth. "Nothing. It's an area of study I got into in college. Earned my Masters in the fall and will be starting my Ph.D. this summer. I took the spring semester off to focus on... other things."

The walls of the greenhouse appeared through the trees. Lelindia stood on the front steps, waving at them. "Hurry up!" she called out.

Brendan chuckled. "She really loves that greenhouse."

"Yes, she does." She pulled her hand away from his to fetch the key from her pocket, unlocking the door to let Lelindia inside.

She and Brendan followed, the plants in the enclosed space greeting her with a warm, moist hug. She sighed, allowing the touch of their energy to fill her with the sense of peace and belonging she craved.

"Wow."

She turned.

Brendan stood, eyes wide, as he surveyed his surroundings. "I thought your bedroom was impressive, but this..." His arms opened to encompass the room. "I've never seen so many plants in one place."

The awe in his voice warmed her more than the greenhouse. His reaction was even better than she'd hoped. "I'm glad you like it."

"Like it?" He looked at her. "I *love* it. You did all this?"

"Me and Marina. She's more into the edible plants, while I like the decorative ones."

His gaze swept the room again. "I recognize a few, but I could use a guided tour." The light in his eyes made her breath catch.

"We gotta pot the plants." Lelindia's voice and the tug of her small hand broke the spell.

Libra glanced down. "Yes, we do. Let's show Brendan where we keep the pots."

"Okay!" She skipped down the nearest aisle, headed for the back wall.

Brendan stepped closer, lowering his voice as they followed Lelindia through the greenhouse. "Is she always this energetic?"

She coughed into her hand to cover the sharp inhalation his question had triggered. *Energetic* was a loaded word for her. "Um, yes. She's a very energetic child." He didn't know the half of it.

And she'd just realized she'd created a problem for herself by letting Lelindia come with them. If Brendan could see *her* energy field, there was a good chance he'd be able to see Lelindia's, too. She'd have to keep him distracted while Lelindia transferred the seedlings to their new containers.

Crouching in front of the shelf that held their spare pots, she helped Lelindia select the ones they needed, moving them to the adjustable potting bench. She lowered the work surface so Lelindia could reach it.

Brendan helped her fetch the herb seedlings from the batch in the center row, lining them up on the bench.

"Okay, Lelindia, I'm going to leave you to repot the plants while I give Brendan a tour of the greenhouse, okay?"

Lelindia's eyes widened slightly. And no wonder. She'd never worked unsupervised before. This was a big step. But she accepted the opportunity with her usual enthusiasm. "Okay!"

Not that there was any risk other than a broken pot or two. Lelindia could heal any damage she accidentally inflicted on the seedlings. No, the real danger was in letting Brendan see the emerald green energy field the child produced when she worked with plants.

"Have fun." She gave Lelindia an encouraging smile before placing her hand on Brendan's back and turning him in the opposite direction.

"You don't want to help her?" he asked, starting to look over his shoulder.

She caught the glow of Lelindia's field out of the corner of her eye and immediately tugged him forward, drawing his gaze away. "It's a good growth opportunity for her." Another idea popped out of her mouth before her brain gave it much thought. "And it gives us some time alone."

He halted, his startled expression confirming she'd taken him by surprise. "I guess it does." He stepped closer. Judging by the look in his eyes, and the way his gaze dropped to her mouth, he was considering kissing her.

His lips reminded her of burgundy rose petals. Would they feel as soft and silky?

She wanted to find out, but she couldn't guarantee Lelindia wouldn't notice. And interrupt them. If Brendan was going to kiss her, she wanted to be alone with him so she could enjoy it.

He met her gaze, his losing the focused intensity, almost like he was reacting to her thoughts.

She backed up a step.

Could he read her thoughts? He could see her energy field. What else was he picking up from her?

A puzzled look crossed his face. "Is something wrong?"

Not a mind reader, then. But possibly intuitive. Certainly more aware than any Human she'd met. She'd have to watch herself. "Not a thing."

She reached for his hand, capturing it in hers and drawing him to the far aisle, keeping his back to the potting bench and his focus on the plants.

Eight

Libra was the most puzzling woman Brendan had ever encountered. One moment she was looking at him like she wanted to eat him up with a spoon, and the next she acted as skittish as a newborn fawn.

Her emotional swings matched her behavior, which made her even more of an enigma. He'd met plenty of people whose words said one thing while their emotions revealed the truth, but even though Libra was clearly hiding something from him, she wasn't lying. In fact, part of her anxiety seemed to be coming from her desire *not* to lie to him.

Which made him want to peel back the layers and learn more.

She took her time leading him down the far aisle of the greenhouse, describing the various plants along the way. It had to be a trick of the mind, but he swore he could practically see the plants reaching out toward her as she passed, growing before his eyes.

He was unfamiliar with most of them, but he could tell these were very healthy specimens. Everything in the greenhouse vibrated with life. The sensation reminded him of how he'd felt as a teenager during an expedition he'd taken with his parents to the rainforest. The lifeforce of the plants had been tangible there, too.

Libra was a delightful teacher, enthusiastic about her subject, growing more animated the longer she talked. He soaked up every word, intensely aware of the subtle caress of her fingers on his hand. He'd been sorely tempted to kiss her more than once, but the tenor of her emotions told him it wasn't the right time. Soon. But not yet.

He caught her taking surreptitious glances over his shoulder in the direction of the potting bench where Lelindia was working. A low-grade anxiety ran underneath her more buoyant emotions, making it clear she wasn't as calm about leaving the little girl alone with her task as she'd claimed. Still, he agreed with her decision. Kids needed to learn responsibility by being given responsibility. And he hadn't heard the crash of broken pottery or a cry of alarm, so Lelindia had to be doing okay.

"How long have you had a fascination with plants?"

Libra smiled. "Since birth. Marina tells a story about a flowering vine that grew beside my cradle. It wound around the frame until I was surrounded by greenery. Apparently I'd lie there and stare at it for hours, reaching out to touch the leaves."

He grinned. "I can picture that. A little fairy princess, lying amongst the flowers."

Her smile faltered, a shadow passing through her emotional field as she turned away.

He drew her back toward him. "What did I say?"

She shook her head but didn't look at him. "It's nothing."

"Libra, please tell me."

She drew in a shuddering breath. When she lifted her gaze, her eyes glimmered with unshed tears. "I miss my parents."

Her pain and sense of loss hit him in the solar plexus like a punch. Deep, powerful, raw. A single teardrop rolled down her pale cheek.

He brushed it away with his thumb, his sadness blending with hers. "It's been two years since my parents died in the earthquake, but I still miss them every day. I'm not sure that ache ever disappears. Maybe it isn't meant to."

She searched his gaze, as if looking for answers to questions she didn't know how to ask. "Maybe not."

But it was meant to abate over time. The force of her emotions stunned him. After so many years, they shouldn't be this strong. Which indicated she'd bottled them up rather than facing them.

And likely turned herself into an emotional powder keg in the process.

She needed help. He could feel it. Would she let him—

"I'm done!"

Lelindia's happy squeal snapped his head around.

She came bounding down the aisle toward them. "Come look, Sahzade!" She grabbed Libra's hand and pulled her forward.

"Sahzade?" he asked as he followed them back up the aisle.

She waved the question away without turning. "It's a nickname."

So she claimed, but he'd caught her tremor of alarm when Lelindia had said it. Like everything else about Libra, there appeared to be much more below the surface than what she was showing him.

When Lelindia reached the potting bench, she swept her arms out, like a barker announcing a big show. "All done."

Brendan grinned as he surveyed the results. The seedlings had made it safely into their new pots and seemed none the worse for wear. But there was easily as much soil on the bench as in the pots. Maybe more.

Libra crouched down to inspect the seedlings. "Great job! If you hand them to me one at a time, we'll get them back on the racks."

He stood aside as the two worked together. Libra showed infinite patience as Lelindia carefully lifted each pot and placed it in her hands before moving on to the next one. When the task was complete, Libra moved the soil bin up to the edge of the table and handed Lelindia a small whisk broom, letting her sweep the spilled soil into the bin. Which mostly worked, although a few bits drifted onto the floor.

The longer he watched, the more entranced he became. He'd already figured out Gryphon and Marina were good parents. Lelindia was a great kid. Now he knew Libra would be a good parent, too.

That shouldn't matter to him. He'd just met her.

But it did.

"Well done." Libra held her hand up for a high-five, and Lelindia smacked it before turning to him.

"Wanna see my room?"

He laughed. She was too cute not to. "I'd like that, but first I need to go with your dad to check on my plane. Maybe when I get back?"

She nodded like they'd just closed an important deal. "Okay." Then she skipped down the aisle toward the door.

They followed her out. The mood had shifted, so he didn't take Libra's hand this time, but he still enjoyed walking beside her down the path to the cabin. He inhaled the fresh, evergreen-scent of the trees. "Marina's right. This place is amazing."

She glanced up at him with a smile. "Yes, it is. I can't imagine wanting to live anywhere else."

Her comment caught him off guard. "Really? Nowhere else?"

She shook her head, her gaze sweeping the trees. "This is perfect."

Perfect. Hard to argue against that. But it put him in a tough spot. "What about a gorgeous tropical beach, like Hawaii?" A not-at-all-random example.

She flinched, the shadow returning to her emotional field. "I don't like the beach."

Oh, boy. The formerly level ground he'd been walking started to look like a rugged mountain pass. She didn't like flying, and now she didn't like the beach. All she needed to say next was she didn't like people with money, and he'd have the trifecta. "Have you ever been to Hawaii?"

"No." And the flatness in her tone made it clear she didn't want to go.

"There are a lot of beautiful plants there. Vibrant flowers in a rainbow of colors." Yes, he was playing dirty, but he needed a lifeline, some hope he wasn't barreling toward a brick wall.

She gave him a sidelong glance, her brows drawing down. "Is that where you live? Hawaii?"

"It's where I grew up. And I have a house there." One of several, not all on Earth. But the house on Diamond Head had been his parents' favorite, and his, too.

"Oh." The sadness returned, along with a sense of confusion, like she was wrestling with herself.

He dove into the breach. "But I travel a lot, so it's not like I spend all my time there." He gestured to the cabin as it appeared on their right. "I could see having a house in this area, too."

"Too?" Her confusion tipped toward anxiety.

He didn't want to risk hitting that trifecta. Not in the space of an hour. "Something small, a cozy cabin like this one. Rustic. Homey." He was blathering, but he couldn't stop himself. It felt like the connection they'd made earlier was dissolving.

"Hmm." Her frown remained, but she didn't pursue the point.

Neither did he.

Gryphon was waiting for them outside the front door. "Ready to check out the plane?" His eyes narrowed as he noted Libra's frown. The look he shot Brendan wasn't encouraging.

"Sure." He needed some time to lick his wounds and come up with a new game plan.

Libra paused at the door, looking back at him, uncertainty surrounding her like a cloud. "I'll see you later?"

He smiled, although it took some effort. "We won't be gone long."

She didn't smile back, just nodded and slipped inside.

Gryphon turned his back to the door and folded his arms, his voice low. "What did you do?"

He'd lost every millimeter of goodwill he'd gained during breakfast. "Nothing. We were talking about the forest, how much she liked it here, and then I mentioned Hawaii. She just kinda shut down, said she didn't like the beach and got really quiet."

Gryphon's ice wall cracked, understanding dawning in his emotional field. His arms dropped to his sides. "Come on." He motioned for Brendan to follow. "Let's talk on the way."

That was the most promising thing he'd heard from his host so far.

He followed him down the hill in front of the house, where a narrow trail wound through the trees. They walked in silence for about a minute, the trees shutting out the view of the cabin.

Gryphon slowed as they climbed a small rise and headed down the opposite side. "You stepped on a land mine with Libra, asking about Hawaii. She has a very negative association with tropical beaches."

"So I gathered. Why?"

"That's her story to tell. Suffice to say you won't earn any points by bringing it up. And she'll never agree to go there."

Never was a strong word. Whatever trauma she'd suffered, he could help her. And Gryphon now seemed inclined to point out the hazards of the road, rather than trying to run him off it. "Is her trauma related to her parents' deaths?"

Gryphon hesitated before answering. "Yes."

"Can you tell me how they died?"

"No."

A flicker in Gryphon's emotional field made him analyze that one-word response closely. "No, because you aren't willing to, or no because you don't know?"

"No, because some things need to stay buried in the past."

"That doesn't work."

Gryphon halted, turning to face him. "What?"

"Burying emotions, refusing to deal with trauma, it doesn't work. The conscious mind may believe it's okay, but the subconscious knows the truth. Over time, suppressing emotions will eat away at a person—mentally, emotionally, physically—until the trauma rises to the surface and manifests as disease."

Gryphon frowned. "Are you a doctor?"

"Not yet, but I just finished my masters in psychology, with an emphasis on the mind-body connection."

"You said you work in aerospace." Not quite an accusation.

"I do. That's my other passion."

"When do you sleep?"

The tone of the question was off. It took him a couple seconds to figure out Gryphon was teasing him. And another second to see the spark of amusement in his eyes.

He made a soft lob back to test the waters. "Never when I'm flying."

The hint of a smile softened Gryphon's rugged features. "Glad to hear it, boy."

Boy? Not a term anyone had applied to him in fifteen years or more, but he wasn't about to object if Gryphon wanted to call him that. In fact, he could call him anything he wanted as long as he kept helping him figure out the enigma that was Libra.

Which brought up another question. "What's Libra's last name?"

Gryphon turned and started walking again. "Hawke, with an e."

Libra Hawke. Pretty, but the last name didn't fit. Maybe it was her perpetual low-grade anxiety and sadness that made him think of a wounded dove or sparrow, rather than a hawk. And her desire to hide in the shadows. Or behind a tree. Hawks didn't hide unless they were hunting. Or protecting their nests.

"Has she ever gotten help from someone, to work through her trauma?"

"No."

"Have you encouraged her to?"

Gryphon sighed. "Look, Brendan, I know you're trying to help. And you're asking valid questions that show you care. But Libra's situation is... special. Nobody around here's going to be able to help her."

"Then I could bring someone in. Just tell me what she needs and I'll arrange it."

Gryphon stopped again, his jaw flexing. "Just like that? Snap your fingers and someone will do your bidding? Do you throw money around like this all the time?"

That stung. He squared his shoulders, looking Gryphon in the eye. "I'm not throwing money around. I'm offering a solid solution that will help Libra overcome whatever trauma is trapping her in a state of emotional suppression. Don't you want that for her?"

Gryphon held his gaze, a new emotion pushing to the forefront. Hope. "More than you'll ever know."

"Then let me help her. If you don't think she'd be comfortable talking to a professional, then I could work with her in an unofficial capacity."

"What about your job? Don't you need to get back?"

"Actually, I don't. I was flying down to San Diego to participate in an air show, but after that, I was scheduled to start my vacation, first one I've had in years. I could just as easily spend that time here."

Gryphon's brows lifted. "Here?"

"Not *here*, here." He didn't want Gryphon to think he was inviting himself to stay at the cabin. "But I could get a room in the nearest town and drive out each day. Or as often as Libra's willing to have me." The more he talked about it, the more he liked it.

"I don't think that's a good idea."

"Why not?"

"Because that would give Libra time to think. And when she thinks, she obsesses. If you're serious about doing this, you'll need to stay at the cabin. You can sleep on the couch."

It took him a moment to pick his jaw off the ground. "Couch, floor... hell, put me in the broom closet for all I care. I just want a chance."

"A chance to help her?"

"You know it's more than that."

"I do, but I wanted to hear you say it. What exactly are your intentions?"

Had Gryphon really just asked him that? It sounded like a line from an old movie. But a serious one. And he needed a serious answer.

Digging into the core of his emotions, he gave the most honest answer he could. "I want to bring her joy, any way that I can, for as long as she'll let me."

"And if that's fifteen minutes?"

"I'll tell her how I feel, but if we're not on the same page, I'll go." It physically hurt to say the words, but he meant it. If his presence wasn't adding to Libra's happiness, he'd leave.

Gryphon studied him for several long moments. "You're an unusual man."

"And she's an unusual woman."

"Which should make this very interesting."

Nine

As they drew closer to the location of the crash, Brendan could smell the acrid odor of spilled engine oil and fuel. The scent prepared him for what he'd find when they stepped out of the trees and onto the service road.

Romeo sat—mostly intact—at the base of a giant redwood. The nose and wing on the passenger side both looked like they'd taken a punch from a giant, while the wing on the other side had crumpled on impact with the tree. The leaked fuel had come from that wing, the oil from the engine.

Broken branches and bark littered the area around the plane. They crunched under his feet as he reached the passenger side and ducked under the wing. "Hey, Romeo." He rested a hand on the plane's side, his throat tightening as he knelt, surveying the scope of the damage from every angle.

Worse than he'd hoped, but not as bad as he'd feared. Most people would write the plane off as a loss, but he wasn't about to let that happen. Not with the resources he could bring to bear on the problem. "Don't worry." He patted the dented wing. "I'll get you fixed up like new."

"Is it worth the effort?"

He turned to face Gryphon, a flare of irritation making him plant his hands on his hips. "To me it is. This plane has been in my family for generations. My great-great-great-great-great grandmother was the original owner."

Gryphon's brows lifted, his gaze moving over the plane like he was seeing it with new eyes. "Is that so?" His emotional field altered as the seconds ticked by, his gaze finally zeroing in on Brendan again. "This aerospace company you work for. By any chance do you own it?"

He hadn't given Gryphon enough credit for astute observation. "Yes, I do."

Gryphon gave a slow-motion nod, like all the pieces were coming together in his head. "That explains a lot."

"It's not a fact I usually hide, but Libra had a negative reaction when I mentioned aerospace so—"

"What do you mean, negative reaction? She didn't say anything."

"She didn't have to. I could feel her emotional reaction."

Gryphon's brows climbed toward his hairline. "You can feel emotions?"

"Yes. I'm an empath. The ability runs in my family."

Gryphon chewed on the idea. "You're telling me you've known what all of us have been feeling this entire time?"

The question didn't come out nearly as harshly as it could have. "Yes. It's how I knew you didn't want me at the cabin, but

Marina did. How I knew Libra was nearby, hiding behind a tree. And how I know without a doubt that she's drawn to me, just like I'm drawn to her."

Gryphon folded his arms, but it was a casual gesture, like he was settling in for the discussion. "How does she feel about that? Being drawn to you, I mean?"

Not the reaction he'd expected. And an unusual question. He gave it some consideration. "Confused. Excited. Wary. Most of the time she seems to be holding herself back, although I get the feeling it's not the attraction that worries her. It's something else, maybe something tied to her past trauma."

Gryphon's expression and emotional field didn't give any indication of whether he was on target.

"Care to throw me a bone on that one? I'm flailing in the dark here."

Gryphon shrugged. "This is between you and Libra. What she chooses to share with you, or not share with you, is up to her. I can tell you that this is new territory for her. And that she's extremely cautious when it comes to anything new, especially new people. Gaining her trust could take a loooong time."

"How long?"

"I honestly don't know. Weeks, months, years."

Years?

Gryphon's gaze turned sympathetic. "You may think I'm trying to scare you off, and earlier you would have been right. Now I want you to go into this with your eyes wide open. Libra deserves someone who's going to be there for the long haul. If you're not prepared for that possibility, then we need to get you back on your way before anyone gets hurt."

"You mean before Libra gets hurt."

"I mean everyone, you included. I believe your intentions are good, but my family has worked hard to find joy in this world. I don't want an ill-conceived plan involving Libra to ruin that."

Gryphon was hiding something, too. He could feel the pressure of it straining his emotional balance. But was it the same secret Libra was holding onto? Or something else? "Do you trust me?"

"I trust that your heart's in the right place. That you want what's best for Libra. But I'm not convinced that what's best for her is you."

"Why not?"

"Because you come from two different worlds. Understanding her—truly understanding who she is and what she needs—may be beyond what you're capable of giving."

"What if you're wrong?"

A grin transformed Gryphon's angular features. "Boy, I would *love* for you to prove me wrong."

Ten

By the time Gryphon and Brendan returned from checking on the plane, Libra was ready to crawl out of her skin. Part of her couldn't wait for them to get back, the part that delighted in the touch of Brendan's hand on hers, the warmth in his eyes, the sound of his voice.

But the part of her that had been calling the shots since she was a child still wanted to run and hide. Brendan's presence had unlocked the door to memories she'd shoved into her mental dungeon, never to be released.

When he'd mentioned the beach, she'd flashed on an image of playing in the aquamarine surf of Feylahn with Marina, splashing each other, riding the waves. Their mothers had watched from the sand, cooing over her baby sister Kreestol with happy smiles.

They'd all been happy then. She'd been carefree and energetic, like Lelindia. And so, so naïve.

She'd had no idea a malevolent force would soon arrive and destroy her world.

A shudder passed through her, the mister of water in her hand slipping through her fingers. She caught it before it hit the floor, but the shaking didn't stop. Sinking to her knees, she touched the leaves of the potted fern and engaged her energy field. The pearlescent glow surrounded the plant, nurturing it, feeding it. Its leaves stretched and unfurled, the touch of its lifeforce calming her, grounding her.

She maintained the connection until the shaking stopped. But when she heard the creak of the front door and the murmur of Brendan's voice, a different tremor took hold.

Rising, she set the bottle on the shelf across from her unmade bed. She'd stripped off the sheets and put them in the washer, although when she'd discovered Brendan's scent still lingered, she'd been tempted to leave them.

His voice drew closer. "Is it okay if I contact Mary Kay?"

"Go ahead," Gryphon responded.

Mary Kay? Creeping toward the doorway, she halted just out of view of the comm panel.

"How's Romeo?" the woman who answered his call asked without preamble.

"Not great, but I'll get him back in the air. I'm sending you the coordinates for the forest service road so the flatbed can retrieve him."

"So you were able to land on the road?"

"I was, but someone else was on the road, too. I saw a shape and the flash of headlights. I must have instinctively turned to avoid a head-on collision and struck a tree."

Headlights. So that's what he thought her shield had been.

"Struck a tree? Are you sure you're okay?"

Her concern drove a shard of guilt into Libra's chest.

"I'm fine. I don't know about the other vehicle. They didn't stop. But some good Samaritans who live nearby found me and took me in for the night."

"Thank goodness for that. I don't know what I would have done if something had happened to you."

The guilt dug deeper.

"If you give me the address, I'll send a chariot to pick you up."

Chariot? She'd never heard of such a thing.

"Actually, I think I'm going to stay put for a while."

Her pulse picked up the pace. He was staying?

Mary Kay's question echoed hers. "You're staying?"

"I've decided to start my vacation here."

Libra started to hyperventilate. Joy and anxiety butted heads in her chest. She leaned against the wall for support.

Mary Kay was silent for a moment. "Brendan, honey, are you sure you're okay?"

A surge of jealousy knocked joy and anxiety down with one punch. Where did this woman get off calling him *honey?*

Brendan chuckled, the rich sound wrapping around her like an embrace. "I'm fine, Mary Kay, I promise. I just think some quiet time here is exactly what I need."

Quiet time *here*, or quiet time with *her?*

"Well, if you're sure."

"I am." The timbre of his voice sent a tingle over her skin.

"Do you need anything?"

"Not right now. I was able to pull my bags out of the plane, so I should be fine for a week or two at least."

A week or two? She gulped and closed her eyes, focusing on keeping the air flowing in and out of her lungs. What had she gotten herself into?

"Then I'll send you a message when the flatbed's on its way. Is tomorrow morning soon enough, or do you want them out today?"

"Tomorrow's fine. Romeo's not going anywhere."

"I assume you'll want to be there when he's loaded?"

"You assume correctly."

"Then I'll let them know to expect you."

"Thank you, Mary Kay."

"You're welcome."

Libra listened for any parting endearments, but didn't hear anything except the soft beep of the connection closing.

Which put her in an awkward spot. If she left the room now, Brendan would know she'd been eavesdropping. But if she didn't, and he asked Marina where she was, she'd be caught, anyway.

His next words gave her an out. "Now that I have my things, I think I'll go brush my teeth. They're feeling a little furry." His footsteps moved further into the living room, followed by rustling, then he walked past the opening near her door and down the hall.

As soon as he closed the bathroom door, she slipped out of her room and into the kitchen, where Gryphon and Marina had set out the baking supplies.

"He's staying?" she whispered, cornering Gryphon as he stirred a pan of melting chocolate on the stove. "Why?"

Amusement danced in his hazel eyes. "You heard him. He's taking his vacation here."

She stared at him. "And you're okay with that?" A few hours ago Gryphon had wanted to get Brendan out the door as quickly as possible. And she'd agreed with him.

Gryphon shrugged. "He's growing on me."

He was growing on her, too. That was part of the problem.

She glanced toward the living room and lowered her voice. "What about what he can see?"

His gaze turned serious. "He thinks he saw headlights. As long as you don't show him your energy field, he'll keep believing that."

"What about Lelindia? He almost saw her field while we were in the greenhouse."

He straightened. "I hadn't thought of that."

Marina moved over to join them. "I have. And I don't think it matters. The real question we should be asking is *why* he can see our fields. Rather than concealing them, I'd like an answer to that question. Then we can better assess the risk of how often we might encounter others who can."

Gryphon's brows drew down. "You trust him enough to get into it?"

Marina nodded. "I do."

Gryphon glanced at her. "What about you?"

"I... don't know. Maybe. I'll think about it."

The creak of the bathroom door opening broke up their huddle. She retreated to the counter and pulled down the teapot, on the pretext of making tea, but stopped when Lelindia's voice halted Brendan in the hallway.

"Come inside!"

Apparently she'd waylaid him, wanting to show him her room.

"You bet."

Their voices grew less distinct as they moved into Lelindia's room at the corner of the house.

Which brought up another point she needed to clarify. "Where will he be sleeping?"

Gryphon glanced at her. "On the couch."

Oh.

He studied her for a moment. "Did you think he'd be sleeping in your room?"

"No. Not exactly. But—"

He set down the wooden spoon he'd been using to stir and faced her. "Do you want him to sleep with you?"

An interesting question. She hadn't allowed her mind to follow that particular trail to its logical conclusion. "No, you're right. The couch is a better option." Even though the idea of Brendan's warm body stretched out beside hers enticed her.

She glanced in the direction of Lelindia's room. "I think I'll go check on them."

Gryphon's lips twitched. "Okay."

She wasn't fooling him, and she didn't care. She had bigger issues on her mind.

Lelindia's voice drifted toward her as she walked down the hallway. "...finded by the creek. It has black marks."

"It's lovely."

Libra paused in the bedroom doorway.

Lelindia had pulled out her treasure trove of rocks. Brendan sat on the floor beside her bed while she carefully lifted each stone out of the wooden box Gryphon had made for her. She'd lined the stones up parallel to Brendan's crossed legs.

He looked up. "Hi, there."

Butterflies fluttered in her stomach. "Hi."

"Lelindia's showing me her rock collection."

"I see that."

Lelindia hopped up and grabbed her hand. "Come sit."

"All right." Libra allowed herself to be led forward, settling in beside Brendan.

Lelindia returned to her spot and reached into the box, drawing out another stone, holding it reverently. "This one has turkeys."

Brendan glanced at Libra with a bemused smile. "Turkeys?"

"Turquoise," she clarified.

"Ah, yes." He reached for the whitish stone with seams of blue-grey, giving it the attention Lelindia's reverence deserved. "Beautiful color." His gaze slid to Libra. "Matches your eyes."

The butterflies took flight, making her lightheaded.

He winked at her before placing the stone in line with the others and focusing on Lelindia.

She couldn't focus on Lelindia at all. That one look had attuned her entire being to Brendan—the steady rise and fall of his chest, the soft rumble of his voice, the electric feeling when his knee brushed hers. If Lelindia hadn't been there, she might have given in to the insane urge to crawl into his lap.

Which is why she noticed the small smile that curved his mouth when she deliberately brushed her knee against his. Despite his attention to the stones, he seemed to be as aware of her as she was of him. An exciting prospect. And a little scary.

Taking advantage of the distraction Lelindia provided, she studied his profile. What was it about him that drew her so strongly? Oh, he was handsome. No doubt about that. His strong jaw, full mouth, and captivating blue eyes would win the admiration of any artist. And his long-sleeved shirt fit snugly enough to stimulate her imagination regarding the toned muscles underneath.

But she'd seen attractive, muscular men at the farmers market plenty of times, and never felt a visceral tug she couldn't explain. Brendan was different. When he'd opened his eyes and looked at her for the first time, she'd felt an instant connection, like seeing a familiar face in a crowd. If it wasn't impossible, she'd wonder if he was Suulh, not Human.

His gaze shifted, meeting hers. A jolt went through her, her breath catching.

His breath wasn't steady and relaxed anymore, either. The intensity in his eyes held her as strongly as iron and as gently as a feather. A yearning built deep inside, but for what she wasn't sure.

"Wanna play cards?"

Brendan cleared his throat, his gaze moving back to Lelindia, who had gathered up her rock collection and set it aside, replacing it with a deck of cards. "What do you want to play?"

His voice held a husky note she hadn't heard before. It did funny things to her heartbeat.

"Slap Jack!"

Brendan chuckled. "That's an oldie but goodie." He glanced at her. "Will you play?"

An excuse to keep sitting beside him? Easy question. "Sure."

Lelindia pulled the cards out of the holder and shuffled them the best way her small hands could, by placing stacks on the floor and then piling them back up. When she was satisfied, they each drew a card to see who would be the dealer. Lelindia drew an eight, Brendan had a five, and she had a two, making her the dealer.

Gathering up the stack, she quickly dealt out all fifty-two cards in three neat piles, then turned to Brendan. "You're first."

His eyes sparkled. "Are you a competitive person?"

He didn't know the half of it. "You'll find out."

Flipping over his top card, he set it in the middle of their small circle. A seven. Lelindia went next with a four, then Libra. They continued around the circle until Lelindia turned over a queen.

She jerked her small hand forward and then back without slapping the deck. "Almost." She shot Libra a grin. "Your turn."

She set down an ace, but Brendan flipped over a jack. They all slapped their hands down on top of it, but Libra was quickest, Lelindia next, with Brendan's hand on top.

His brows lifted as she pulled the stack of cards toward her and shuffled them into her pile. "I guess I have my answer."

She gave him a satisfied smile. "Guess so."

Lelindia claimed the next stack before either Libra or Brendan reacted. But Libra got the third stack, Brendan's hand landing on top of hers. His palm warmed her skin as his thumb stroked hers in a casual caress that totally blew her concentration. She lost the next three jacks to him and Lelindia.

He flicked a glance in her direction after his second win, his smile taunting.

Oh, he wanted to play dirty, did he?

She shifted closer so their knees touched and was rewarded by a sharp inhalation.

She claimed the next two jacks, and Lelindia got the one after that, leaving Brendan with a pathetically small deck. She leaned closer, resting her forearm on top of his thigh as she studied his meager stack of cards. His muscles flexed in reaction to her touch, but she kept her attention on Lelindia. "Should we go easy on him since he's a guest?"

Lelindia's mouth pursed like Libra had said something offensive. "No."

Libra grinned, straightening. "That's my girl. Sorry, Brendan." She fluttered her lashes. "You're going down."

He grinned. "Not without a fight."

Play got fierce after that, but sure enough, Libra knocked Brendan out of the game. He settled back against the bedframe, a soft smile on his face. "I'm going to enjoy seeing how this turns out."

His gaze stayed on her, with predictable results. She couldn't focus on the cards while he was watching her, and Lelindia soon had every card in her plump little hands.

"I win!" she crowed. "Good game," she added, nodding solemnly to Brendan and Libra.

Brendan nodded back, smiling. "Well played."

"Thanks!" She returned the cards to the holder and then paused, sniffing the air audibly. "Brownie time!" She shot out of the room like a cannonball.

Brendan's soft laughter followed her. "Seriously, does she ever slow down?"

She stood. "When she sleeps."

He rose beside her. "Good to know she sleeps."

"Like a rock." An immovable rock who'd pinned her against the wall most of the previous night.

She led the way down the hall to the living room, the scent of baking brownies drifting toward them.

Lelindia was hopping up and down in front of Gryphon. "How soon, Daddy?"

He laughed. "Another fifteen minutes to cool, firefly. Patience."

Libra smiled. Patience wasn't easy to come by for a Suulh child. Lelindia's exuberance was a natural result of all the lifeforce energy continually flowing around her. Humans rarely noticed it, but for a Suulh, the energy of their surroundings was a backup battery that was always fully charged. Suulh children spent their early years learning to balance their own energy fields with all the external input. The training was even more necessary for a daughter of the Nedale or Sahzade, like Lelindia.

She glanced at Brendan, who was also watching Lelindia with a smile. His presence would make Lelindia's training sessions a little trickier, but Marina would figure out a way to keep her on track.

They joined Lelindia as she climbed on one of the barstools at the kitchen peninsula. "Daddy makes the *best* brownies," she informed Brendan.

"They certainly smell good."

Gryphon was in the process of gathering the ingredients for the dark chocolate fudge ganache he drizzled on top. He reached out and snagged Marina around the waist as she moved past him toward the sink. "I learned long ago that the way to a woman's heart is a healthy dose of chocolate." He gave her a kiss on the cheek.

Brendan turned to Libra, a teasing light in his eyes. "Is that true? Is chocolate the secret?"

"For some women." Not her, though. Oh, she liked chocolate, but festive decorations were her weakness. She'd taken down the Christmas wreaths, bows, and lights that had filled the cabin a week ago, but she still had a couple strands of white lights up in her bedroom.

Marina extricated herself from Gryphon's grip. "Libra, would you and Brendan mind restocking the fireplace woodpile? We're supposed to get near freezing tonight. It'd be nice to have a fire going all evening."

She slid off her barstool and walked to the coat tree. "Of course." Normally she wouldn't have bothered grabbing her coat for such a short trek. If she got cold, her energy field would warm her up. But engaging it wasn't an option with Brendan by her side, not unless she wanted to tackle the question Marina had posed.

Not yet.

She plucked her coat off the rack while Brendan grabbed his and pulled it on.

The jacket made his shoulders look even broader. And stronger.

He caught her staring and gave her a slow smile.

Now she *really* didn't need her coat, but she put it on anyway. "Follow me." Leading the way through the front door, she took him around the side of the house to the back, where the woodpile sat under the roof overhang, filling the space between the windows for her bedroom and Marina and Gryphon's.

She snagged two pairs of gloves out of the small toolshed beside the wood, something else she normally wouldn't use since her shield could protect her skin. She handed him Gryphon's while she pulled on Marina's.

Brendan stepped closer, holding his arms out, elbows next to his body. "Load me up."

"All right." She selected a couple larger logs first, placing them across his forearms.

Which brought her into very close proximity to him. When she glanced up, he was watching her. Her heart did a little tap dance. "What?"

"You look beautiful."

She stood very still. "I do?"

"Mm-hmm. In that coat, you really do look like an angel."

"I'm no angel." *Just a visitor from another planet with abilities that would terrify you.*

His eyes narrowed, but the corners of his mouth lifted. "Oh, I know that. I've seen you play Slap Jack."

She laughed, the tension easing. "I play to win." She grabbed a couple smaller logs and added them to his stack.

"I'm glad. I like a little friendly competition."

She placed three smaller logs on top. "Then you'll like me."

"I already do."

She paused, her heartbeat picking up. "I like you, too."

His smile grew. "I know."

Something about the way he said it triggered an alert. She picked up a few logs for herself. "How do you know?"

He nodded toward the front door. "Let's carry this batch inside and I'll tell you when we come back out."

That kept her blood pumping. "Okay." Settling a few smaller logs into the crook of her arm, she led the way back to the front door, holding it open for him as he walked through. After they'd deposited the wood on the rack beside the fireplace, she followed him back out to the woodpile.

He turned and faced her, the angle of the midday sun burnishing his hair with gold. "The reason I know how you feel about me is because I'm an empath."

"An empath? You mean you're compassionate?" She'd seen evidence of that in his dealings with Lelindia.

"I try to be. But it's deeper than that. I can literally feel what other people are feeling."

He could... Fear drove her backward. "You can—"

"Whoa, whoa." He reached for her, grasping her upper arms and halting her retreat. "Please don't be afraid."

Impossible request. She trembled under his touch. He could sense her *feelings?* What had she been telling him without even knowing? What had she revealed?

"I'm sorry, Libra." He drew her closer.

She was too terrified to resist.

"I should have told you sooner." He tucked her against his chest, resting his cheek on top of her head. "Please don't be afraid of me."

His heart was beating almost as fast as hers. Which made her realize he was scared, too. Scared that she would reject him because he had an ability she didn't understand.

Oh, the irony.

"I would never, *ever* hurt you." It was a plea. And a promise.

The warmth of his body soothed her, melting away her fears like hot wax and relaxing her muscles. Slowly, tentatively, she slid her arms around his waist, snuggling her head against his chest.

His breath released on a sigh, his arms tightening around her. "Thank you, Libra. Thank you for your trust."

Gryphon had asked if she trusted him. She hadn't known the answer then, but she did now. She couldn't explain why, even to herself. But understanding he had a special ability made her feel more connected to him, not less. To her, he shone like a star, lighting her world.

It made no sense. But it was real.

Eleven

Brendan hadn't expected his announcement to trigger an avalanche of fear, and Libra's reaction had sliced his heart like a dagger.

He'd reached for her purely on instinct, needing to make physical contact, needing to prove to her that he wasn't a threat. In that moment, he'd realized he would do anything to drive the fear away from her, to keep her safe.

He couldn't even begin to explain why she'd become so important to him in such a short time. But their connection felt elemental, deeper and stronger than anything he'd ever experienced. And her feelings towards him were just as powerful, if a bit confusing.

She stirred in his arms, lifting her head and meeting his gaze. Her blue eyes held a thousand questions. "So... you can feel what I'm feeling, when I'm feeling it?"

"Yes." He brushed a strand of hair away from her cheek. "Although I don't always understand what I'm sensing."

Her gaze searched his, a small frown line forming between her brows. "That seems... invasive."

He winced. "I don't mean it to be. I respect your privacy. But sensing your emotions helps me understand you."

"It also gives you an advantage. You know what I'm feeling, but I don't know what you're feeling."

"Don't you?" Her fear had abated. Now it felt like she was testing the boundaries of their altered dynamic. He could help with that. "I'll bet you know what I'm feeling right now." Rather than sensing her emotions, he projected his own. All of them.

Her frown deepened for a moment, and then her cheeks flushed pink. Her breathing stuttered, too, as awareness lit her eyes. "Yes, I do."

He cradled her cheek in his palm. "Libra, I—"

"Brownies are ready!"

Gryphon's boisterous call from the direction of the front door split them apart like a sledgehammer's blow.

Great timing, Gryphon.

"Be right there," Libra called back, glancing toward the side of the house. She gave him a nervous smile. "We need to take another load of wood."

He nodded. She quickly handed him several logs and then grabbed a few more herself before heading for the door.

The scent of chocolate surrounded them as they walked into the living room. But chocolate wasn't what he was craving. Unfortunately, for now, it would have to do.

After they added the wood to the fireplace rack, he followed Libra to the kitchen sink to wash up. Row upon row of brownies covered the counter. There had to be close to a hundred. "That's a lot of brownies."

"Which I'll be selling at the farmers market tomorrow," Gryphon replied.

"Ah." He dried his hands on the towel beside the sink.

"They're very popular, especially during the winter months." Marina held out a plate and fork. "Would you like one?"

One of the tempting treats sat in the center of the plate, the drizzled ganache creating small pools of chocolate on the sides. "Absolutely." His inner chocoholic had taken command, making his mouth water.

"Wait until you taste it," Libra murmured as she passed him on her way to the barstool beside Lelindia, a matching plate in her hand.

He followed her, claiming the last seat. Three mugs of hot tea already sat along the raised counter, the smallest one next to Lelindia. "Thank you for this." He lifted the plate and gestured to the tea.

Gryphon nodded, his focus on the brownies as he carefully placed them in bakery boxes, while Marina poured a mug of tea for herself. "You're welcome."

Picking up his fork, he cut off a chunk, swirled it in the ganache and took a bite. *Damn!* Rich, chocolate heaven melted in his mouth. It almost made up for the missed moment with Libra.

Well, no. It wasn't *that* good. But still amazing.

Flickers of amusement brushed him from three directions, making him realize he'd closed his eyes. Opening them, he found Gryphon, Marina, and Libra all watching him with nearly identical smiles.

"I take it you like it?" Gryphon asked.

"Oh, yeah. I'll buy one of those packages right now."

Gryphon snorted. "Don't have to. I always make extras to have on hand. Libra's not a chocoholic, but Marina certainly is. And Lelindia hasn't met a sweet treat she doesn't like. They'd never forgive me if I sold all the baked goods."

"I can see why." He took another bite. Yep, just as good. Gryphon would be an exceptional personal chef. "Have you ever considered starting a catering business?"

Gryphon shook his head. "I like cooking in small batches for my family. And baking things for the market. But I'm not interested in making it a career."

"Too bad. You'd have people beating down your door."

Gryphon exchanged a look with Marina, a ripple of unease passing between them that extended out to Libra.

What had he said?

Gryphon turned away. "The market's good enough for us."

He glanced at Marina, then Libra, but they both avoided his gaze. What invisible tripwire had he sprung? He cleared his throat. "Speaking of the market, what time will you be leaving in the morning?"

"Eight," Marina replied, taking a bite of her own brownie.

"And how long are you there?"

"Until one," Libra answered. "Both Saturday and Sunday."

He'd been thinking about going with them, but he wouldn't be able to do that and monitor Romeo's loading. "I'll probably need to stay here tomorrow, but I'd like to go with you on Sunday, if that's okay."

The tension eased out of the room.

Gryphon glanced over and nodded, continuing with his boxing. "We can squeeze you in, as long as you don't mind boxes of baked goods on your lap."

He smiled. "If you keep me stocked with brownies I can eat, I'll do any job you want done."

Gryphon turned, a gleam in his eyes. "Oh, really?"

He couldn't back down now. "Sure."

Gryphon's gaze flicked to Libra, a subtle challenge in his voice. "Glad to hear it, because we still need to gather the produce from the greenhouse. I could use Marina's help in here this afternoon if you'd be willing to go with Libra after lunch."

Gryphon had said the magic words. Go with Libra. "I'd be happy to."

Twelve

Walking to the greenhouse with Brendan this time felt quite different. The sun was already well past its zenith, painting the trees and pathway in shadows. Lelindia wasn't with them, either. As they moved out of sight of the cabin the stillness made Libra acutely aware of their isolation. And the man beside her.

Gryphon's challenge had been meant for her, not Brendan. Sending him with her presented her with an opportunity to make a choice—show him her energy field and deal with the fallout, or continue to struggle to conceal it.

Ordinarily she used her energy field during the harvesting process to keep the plants in the lush, fresh condition their customers were accustomed to. She'd intended to start gathering them this morning but had been too discombobulated to accomplish much of anything.

Brendan's presence would make the process trickier.

That is, unless she accepted Gryphon's challenge and worked up the courage to show Brendan what she could do.

He hadn't taken her hand during the walk, although she was fairly certain he'd considered it. He seemed to be giving her physical and emotional space. "What exactly does gathering the produce entail?" he asked.

"I'll be in charge of harvesting whatever's ready, and you'll be at the washstand, cleaning it up and loading it into the bins."

He nodded. "Sounds simple enough."

Nothing simple about it.

Unlocking the greenhouse, she led the way inside.

Brendan glanced at the key in her hand. "Are you worried someone will break in?"

"Yes. Several furry someones who could have a feast in here. The lock keeps them from pushing open the door."

"Ah. Hadn't thought of that."

"If you spend much time here, you will. We don't see Humans out here very often, but plenty of other critters call this area home."

He cocked his head, staring at her with a strange look on his face.

She quickly replayed what she'd said. And realized her mistake. She'd said Human, rather than people. It was a distinction she, Marina, and Gryphon made with each other all the time. But it obviously sounded odd to Brendan.

Best not to give him a lot of time to think about it. "The washstand is over here." She moved past him to the wood and metal stand in the front corner. "You'll lay the veggies over the mesh to spray them down."

He crouched, looking at the multi-tiered setup and the catch basin at the bottom. "And the water that collects down here?"

"Gets used to irrigate the plants."

"Elegant." He grinned. "I like it."

His grin was infectious, chipping away at her anxiety. "We'll see if you still like it after you've been washing for a couple hours."

"I'm not afraid of hard work." He shrugged out of his jacket and hung it on one of the pegs near the door.

She followed suit.

He pushed back his sleeves. "What's first?"

"Beets." Those would be easiest for her to harvest without using her field because she'd be pulling up the entire plant. And if she did need to use her field, her hands would be buried in the soil where he couldn't see the glow. "Follow me."

She grabbed one of the stainless-steel bins and headed down the aisle. When they reached the beets, she handed him the bin and began working the beets out of the soil, laying them carefully in the bin. Once it was full, she shooed him away. "The tops stay on, so do the best you can to get the soil off. They don't have to sparkle."

He smiled. "Got it."

She kept her back to him as they worked in silence for a while, the whoosh of the sprayer and the rustle of greenery the dominant sounds. Then he started humming softly. She didn't recognize the tune, but the melody brought a smile to her face, especially when the humming turned into singing.

He had a nice voice, like velvet. And perfect pitch. She couldn't catch most of the words, but if he kept singing, she'd be able to reproduce the notes.

As she carried the next load of veggies to the washstand, she listened to the lyrics, which spoke of rain disappearing and sunlight emerging. "What song are you singing?"

He shut off the sprayer and turned. "It's an old tune my parents sang all the time when I was a kid. It's called *I Can See Clearly Now.*"

"Sounds like a happy song."

"It is. I have a tendency to sing to myself whenever I'm working. Was I bothering you?"

"Not at all." She handed him the bin. "You have a great voice."

He took it from her, their fingers brushing. His blue eyes warmed. "Thank you."

And the temperature in the greenhouse shot up ten degrees. "I should start work on the cabbage." She didn't move.

"I should wash the leeks." But rather than turning away, he held her gaze as he set the bin on the stand. Stepping toward her, he closed the gap. "After a short break."

Impossible to mistake the look in his eyes. His gaze drifted to her mouth as the warmth from his body reached out to her.

She licked her lips. "A break would be nice."

His mouth twitched, like he was trying not to laugh. "Oh, it will be a lot better than nice."

Her heart pounded as he circled one arm around her waist, eliminating the tiny space between them. She could feel his heart pounding, too. He wasn't as calm as he seemed.

He lifted his other hand, brushing his knuckles in a feather touch from her jaw to her temple. "You enchant me, Libra."

She trembled as he continued the caress, the pads of his fingers tracing her brow and cheekbone. He tunneled his fingers into her hair and cupped the back of her head, urging her closer. She leaned into his touch, her hands moving of their own volition, gripping his muscled shoulders.

She'd been kissed once before, by Wolf, but his touch hadn't generated the sensations coursing through her veins now. That didn't stop her from recognizing them for what they were. This was desire. At this moment she wanted Brendan's lips on hers more than she wanted her next breath.

The pressure on the back of her head increased as his eyes darkened, his heart thumping in time with hers. His breath brushed her cheek, and then his lips touched down on hers.

That first contact sent a charge through her nerve endings like lightning. The second brush of his soft lips coaxed a moan from her throat. Somehow her fingers ended up tangled in his hair, pulling him closer.

He made a firmer connection, sealing his mouth over hers in a touch that signaled both claiming and surrendering. She responded in kind, rising up on tiptoes to increase the delicious pressure. But when his tongue stroked her lip, her body quaked like a fault line. Warmth flowed over her in a never-ending river, pulling her into a whirlpool of delight.

He groaned, his arms tightening around her, nearly lifting her off her feet. His tongue slipped inside her mouth, blasting all conscious thought into oblivion. He tasted rich and decadent, a heady and potent flavor all his own. She couldn't get enough.

With another groan, he pulled back, breaking the connection. His panting exhalations mingled with hers as he rested his forehead against hers. "You are... an incredible gift." Lifting his head, he gazed down at her. And then his eyes snapped wide.

"You're glowing."

Thirteen

The shimmering pearlescence vanished the moment the words were out of Brendan's mouth. A nanosecond later a blast of fear pummeled him, coming from Libra.

He hadn't imagined it. Couldn't have. Her fear made that obvious. And he'd seen it before, after the crash. But what exactly had he seen?

She pushed against his chest, but he held her close. Now wasn't the time to let her run away like a terrified deer. "Libra, don't. It's okay."

Her emotions begged to differ.

So he did the only thing he could think of. He projected all the incredible emotions she'd inspired in him during their kiss back at her.

She stilled, her breath coming in short bursts as she stared at him in confusion. "What are... I..."

He loosened his grip, holding her in a gentle hug. "I don't just feel the emotions of others. I can also project my own. I'm showing you what I feel when I'm with you."

Her gaze searched his, the fear still swirling, but no longer cresting like a wave. "You're not... afraid?"

His brows lifted. "No. Should I be?"

"I... no."

Some of the tension eased from his shoulders. "I don't know what I saw, but it was beautiful. Just like you." And he was making progress. Her breath was evening out, her tremors subsiding.

He pressed on. "From the moment I saw you, I've felt a connection I can't explain. And whatever that glow was, I think it made our connection stronger."

She didn't disagree. In fact, he sensed tendrils of hope winding their way to the surface of her turbulent emotional field. But her lips pursed. "Most people can't see it."

That made him feel special. And damn lucky. He traced patterns on her back with his fingertips, coaxing her tense muscles to relax. "What did I see?"

His touch was having the desired effect. Emphasis on *desire.* Her blue eyes were getting warmer by the second. But she hesitated before answering. "My energy field."

Good start. He'd studied that topic in school. Metaphysical phenomena fascinated him. "You mean your electromagnetic field, your aura?" He'd never seen an aura before, but he'd also never experienced such an elemental connection with someone, either. It could have expanded the scope of his senses.

The corners of her lips turned down. "Kind of. But I can control it." She looked away, the tension creeping back in.

He didn't want to lose this opportunity. "Would you show it to me again?"

She looked back, her frown deepening. "Why?"

"Why?" He laughed before he could stop himself. "Because it's incredible."

His laughter startled her, her body jolting in his arms. Whatever reaction she'd feared, he wasn't giving it to her. And she didn't seem to know what to make of the reaction she was getting.

"Please, Libra. Trust me." He brushed a soft kiss on her forehead before leaning back to look into her eyes. "I promise I would never betray that trust. Ever."

She held his gaze for a long moment, their breathing slowly coming into sync.

He felt her make the decision before she spoke.

"I trust you."

The glow erupted around her, sparkling like a prism catching the light. He inhaled sharply.

She *was* an angel. Or the goddess Venus in human form. Dazzling.

He lifted a hand, passing it slowly through the glow. It was as ephemeral as the air, but warmth surrounded his hand. And then it spread around his entire body, stealing the air from his lungs as she expanded the field to include him.

This was what he'd felt when he'd kissed her. This subatomic connection, like atoms bonding. It was beyond intoxicating. "Oh, Libra."

He lowered his lips to hers before his brain caught up with his body. Didn't care. As her lush mouth opened to the thrust of his tongue, he lost his mind. The kaleidoscope of sensations her energy field created kept them locked together. All he knew for certain was Libra was with him, as eager for his touch as he was for hers.

Time faded into nothingness. The brush of her fingers, the taste of her mouth, the warmth of her skin filled his senses. And through it all, the pulse of the energy field, an extension of her that embraced him completely, touched him in ways he'd never imagined.

He wanted more. *Needed* more.

But when his hand cupped her breast and she moaned, sanity shouldered its way through.

This was *not* the time. And it certainly wasn't the place. Much as he yearned to strip her down and make love to her, he wanted that moment to be as special and beautiful as she was. She deserved no less. And the floor of the greenhouse did not qualify.

Gulping in air, he lowered his hand to her waist and struggled to gather his wits.

Her energy field faded out, which helped. But her hands were still under his shirt, her palms warm against his chest. Her pale cheeks were flushed pink, her blue eyes shining brighter than stars, her lips plump and rosy from his kisses.

He sighed. She was so damn tempting, challenging his restraint. "I want this. More than I can say." He needed to make that point very clear. "But not here. Not now."

"I understand." Her gaze drifted to the rows of plants. "We still have work to do."

When she said it in that throaty purr, he didn't really care whether the work got done or not. But he didn't want to sabotage her. Or get on Gryphon and Marina's bad side. He'd already seen what that looked like. Not a fan.

And now that he'd experienced the wonder of holding her surrounded by her energy field, he wanted to create the perfect setting for their first time together.

But when she withdrew her hands from his skin, he bit back a growl of frustration. He'd gotten himself into this situation by kissing her, and then asking her to show him her energy field. He still had a lot of questions about that, but those would have to wait, too.

He had a tub full of leeks to wash.

She stepped away, straightening her sweatshirt with a small sigh. That made him smile. At least he wasn't the only one suffering aftereffects.

"How much more do we have to do?" he asked her.

"The cabbage and lettuce are the last." She gave him a sideways glance, her lips thinning for a moment. "It will go quicker if I use my energy field to help extricate the plants without causing damage."

He hadn't expected her to offer up more details about her abilities. It took a moment for him to get the point. "So, if I look your way, I might see the glow?"

She nodded, her mouth still tight. She was worried about his reaction.

Leaning down, he brushed a quick kiss over her lips, forcing himself to pull away before it turned into anything more. "That would be nice."

Her frown vanished, a soft smile in its place.

Much better.

Fourteen

Gryphon arrived at the greenhouse an hour later to help them cart the bins down to the transport. Libra did her best to act casual as they tromped along the path together, but she could tell Gryphon knew something was up. Unfortunately, she couldn't discuss it with him, not with Brendan right behind her.

His response to her energy field had shocked her, especially considering she hadn't even been aware that she'd generated the field when he'd kissed her. It had been completely instinctive, their physical and emotional connection triggering a subconscious desire for an energetic bond.

But rather than being afraid or suspicious when he'd seen and felt the field, he'd seemed intrigued and delighted. She wasn't sure how to handle that.

She needed to tell Marina and Gryphon what she'd done, the sooner the better.

Gryphon opened the back door of the transport, and Libra slid the bin of cabbage onto the bottom rack.

"Leeks can go on the top shelf," Gryphon told Brendan as he placed the bin of beets on the top shelf as well.

"Got it." He peered into the vehicle's interior. "What's in the little brown bags?"

"Those would be the cookies I baked yesterday," Gryphon answered. "Oatmeal raisin and chocolate chip."

"So you offer a variety of baked goods?"

Gryphon nodded. "Depends on my mood. In the fall I'll do pies, and in summer I'll whip up some fruit-based treats. Oh, and Yule logs at Christmas. Those are Libra's favorite."

Brendan grinned at her. "You like the coffee and chocolate mix, huh?"

His smile warmed her from the inside out. "I do, but I like the look of them even more than the taste. Gryphon frosts them to resemble tree branches, and I decorate them with edible cinnamon-flavored faux holly sprigs."

"Then I'm going to guess you're responsible for all the winter-themed decorations in the cabin, too."

"You'd be right," Gryphon answered, closing up the vehicle. "Libra can make the most mundane items beautiful."

"I believe you." Brendan's gaze stayed on her, the look in his eyes doing funny things to her breathing.

But he'd also reminded her of another item she needed to have ready for tomorrow. "Speaking of which, I need to put together the wreath Dee requested last week." And which she'd completely forgotten about when Brendan had dropped into her life. "Can you two finish up while I head into the house?" she asked Gryphon. A few minutes alone with Marina would be helpful, too.

He nodded. "Go ahead. We'll be fine."

Brendan gave her a wink. "See you in a bit."

And just like that, her thoughts focused on their kiss, taking over every working brain cell.

When she walked into the cabin, she found Marina and Lelindia in the kitchen, washing up the baking pans. Marina took one look at her and grabbed a towel, drying her hands as she walked to the living room. "What happened?" she asked in a low voice.

Marina always could read her like a book. "We kissed."

"How was it?"

"Wonderful." Just thinking about it brought a flush of warmth. "But my energy field engaged."

Marina's eyes widened. "It did?" She grinned, but it turned into a grimace. "I should have warned you."

"You knew that would happen?" It was news to her, news she would have liked to have heard in advance.

"I didn't know for sure, just suspected." Her smile crept back in. "But I should have warned you, anyway. Even though he's Human, clearly your Suulh senses react to him like he's a Suulh. Or more specifically, like a potential mate."

Her heart stopped. "A potential mate? What do you mean?"

Marina's mouth tightened, her dark eyes growing serious. "I won't go into the biological details, but it's an adaptation our people developed long ago. It helps us to choose the most compatible mates, the ones who balance and strengthen us and who will enable us to produce the strongest children. What you experienced only occurs when you share an intimate connection with someone your energetic field resonates with."

She stared at Marina. "And that's who I should choose?"

"That's who you have the strongest biological connection with. Ideally, that's also the person you have a strong emotional connection with, too. If not…" She shrugged. "You can ignore the biology and go with your heart."

"Why have I never heard about this before?"

"Because you were a child when we left Feylahn. And I didn't want to put any added pressure on you since you have so few options for a Suulh mate."

Three. She had exactly three unmated Suulh males to choose from, all currently living on Gaia, the first Earth-like planet Humans had colonized. And she didn't want any of them. She wanted Brendan. "But he's Human."

"And biologically we're nearly identical to them. Human or not, your energetic field resonates with his. Which makes him a good candidate for a mate."

Her hand flailed behind her, finally connecting with the edge of one of the dining chairs. "I need to sit down." It was either that or fall down. Her knees weren't willing to support her anymore.

Marina pulled out the chair beside her, then took Libra's hands in hers. "I know this is overwhelming. And unexpected. But think about the possibilities. You might be able to have a family with someone you're passionate about, rather than someone you view as a friend."

She was talking about Wolf. She'd never felt anything remotely like this when he was around her. Or when he'd kissed her. "But he's Human." She kept echoing herself but couldn't seem to stop.

"And he can see your energy field. That's why I wanted you to spend time with him. Our energy fields don't lie. If his touch summoned your field during a kiss, you two could conceive a child together."

Libra turned her head, her gaze settling on Lelindia. She was standing on a stepstool beside the sink so she could reach the counter. She picked up one of the baking pans and carefully dried it with a towel.

Conceive a child? With a Human?

For all recorded time, the daughters of the Sahzade and Nedale had always been born in a set pattern, the Nedale first, then the Sahzade, growing up like bonded sisters. Marina and Gryphon had held off having a child until Libra had reached adulthood, but once Lelindia had been born, the pattern had been set in motion. Lelindia would be four in a couple months, which was another reason Wolf had made his intentions known during his last visit. Libra was now old enough to conceive a daughter of her own, to produce an energy sister for Lelindia. The next Sahzade.

"How did Brendan react to seeing your field again?"

"He was fascinated."

"Not upset?"

"Not at all. He liked it."

"Another good sign." Marina squeezed her hand. "You never said anything after Wolf's last visit. Did he kiss you?"

She nodded. "But it wasn't... we didn't..."

"No reaction?"

"No." And now that she'd experienced what Brendan brought to the table, she realized how much of a non-reaction she'd had to Wolf's touch. "I don't want to mate with Wolf."

The admission surprised her. She'd accepted their mating as inevitable long ago, since he was the best option available to her. But she didn't have any romantic feelings for him. Or any attraction. He was like an older brother.

Finally admitting the truth felt a lot like leaping off a bridge.

Marina's dark eyes danced with excitement. "It looks like the universe is offering you a better option."

Her skin tingled with remembered pleasure. If Brendan were her mate, then...

Thinking of him kicked in her internal tracking, alerting her that he and Gryphon were heading back to the cabin. "They're coming." She pushed to her feet. "I need to start on the wreath for Dee."

Marina stood, too. "And I need to finish cleaning up the kitchen before dinner."

While Marina headed for the kitchen, Libra hastily pulled a wreath frame and a spool of winter-themed ribbon from the storage cabinet in the corner, then darted into her room before Brendan and Gryphon came through the door.

The tromp of their footsteps and hearty laughter made her insides dance. She sat on the edge of her bed, taking slow, deep breaths.

Was it possible? Could she conceive a child with a Human? And if she did, would that child have Suulh abilities?

Marina would be able to answer that question better than she could. But she'd said energy fields didn't lie. If her elemental connection to Brendan was that strong, surely her Suulh abilities would pass on to her daughter as well.

And what if they didn't? Did it matter? The slow extinction of her race was a foregone conclusion, no matter what she did. Nine adults couldn't sustain the species.

If they were Human, they might stand a chance. But Suulh couldn't produce large families. Most Suulh females had one or two children. Three was rare, and four was unheard of. And even if Marina somehow found a way to overcome the biological restrictions, Suulh abilities grew considerably weaker with each child conceived. If a fourth child was produced, it wouldn't have any energy abilities. Neither would any children that child conceived.

Which made Lelindia incredibly precious. She was the most powerful Nedale the race would ever have.

Marina hadn't made a point of it during their discussion, but her reaction to the bonding Libra had experienced with Brendan made it clear her connection with Gryphon was just as strong. Which is why they had produced a child with extraordinary abilities. Marina was a great healer, but even now, it was clear Lelindia would far surpass her mother.

But if Libra's odds of finding a Suulh mate who resonated with her were astronomically low, Lelindia's were non-existent. She was the only child who had been born since they'd left Feylahn. And by the time she was of age to conceive a child, Wolf, River, and Leo would be past their reproductive period.

She stared at the wall, the timeline playing out in her mind's eye. If she didn't choose Wolf, he would be free to mate with Skye, Amethyst, or Oracle. So would Leo and River. Which would give Lelindia a better chance at having a Suulh mate. It was the only way for the strength of the Nedale line to continue.

But would you be sacrificing the Sahzade line?

It was a possibility. They were in unexplored territory. Marina was optimistic, but even she couldn't give any guarantees. A Suulh had never tried to mate with a Human before. And there would be no second chances. If she and Brendan mated, the first child they produced would be the strongest, the most powerful of her line. If that child's Suulh abilities were weak, she would have sentenced Lelindia, and all Nedale who followed her, to an existence without a powerful energetic sister to strengthen and protect her.

Was she ready to make that choice?

Fifteen

Brendan had felt Libra's uneasiness as she'd walked into the cabin, but that was nothing compared to what followed. Alternating waves of shock, hope, and anxiety had struck him, challenging his concentration as he'd helped Gryphon carry the remaining bins to the transport.

Gryphon's upbeat attitude had helped, giving him something else to focus on, but as they walked into the cabin, the emotions he'd sensed from Libra spiked. His gaze swept the living room and kitchen, but she wasn't there. Most likely in her bedroom, then. And apparently hiding from him.

What a depressing thought.

In the greenhouse, they'd been so in sync he'd felt like he could almost read her mind. But after Gryphon appeared, Libra had pulled back, leaving him tottering on unsteady ground.

"Where's Libra?" Gryphon asked as he headed for the kitchen.

"In her room, making the wreath for Dee." Marina shot Brendan a look that gave him pause. Her emotions bordered on excitement, and she seemed to be sizing him up, like a shopper picking out a gift from a store display.

What exactly had she and Libra been talking about?

"Well then, Brendan, I guess you'll be helping me with dinner." Gryphon passed Marina and Lelindia at the sink, who were scrubbing baking pans, and began pulling items out of a wire basket on the counter. "Get over here and wash up."

He hesitated. "I'm not sure you want my help."

Gryphon paused, an onion in his hand. "Why not?"

"I don't know how to cook."

Gryphon, Marina, and Lelindia all stopped what they were doing and stared at him. It would have been comical if he wasn't acutely aware of the heat rising up his neck.

"You can't cook?" Gryphon repeated, like the concept was foreign to him.

He shook his head. "But I make a decent PB&J sandwich." He winced as soon as he said it. Lelindia could probably do that.

Gryphon's gaze grew thoughtful. "How does a man your age not learn how to cook?" The look in his eyes indicated he suspected the answer.

And he was right. "I never had to." He'd always had a personal chef at home and on business trips. On shorter hops, like this one with Romeo, he ate out.

"I see." Gryphon exchanged a glance with Marina.

Her lips barely twitched, but he could feel her suppressed laughter.

"Well, boy, I'd say it's high time you learned." Gryphon gestured to the sink. "Wash up."

Gryphon seemed determined to keep calling him boy, despite the fact he was less than ten years older. Two could play that game. "Okay, old man."

A startled look crossed Gryphon's face, but then he grinned, slapping Brendan on the back as he passed.

Gryphon pulled out a cutting board and set him to work chopping the onion, showing him first how to hold the knife to protect his fingers. He also instructed him to run the cut onion under the tap to decrease the burning sensation in his eyes.

Even so, it was slow going. By the time he finished, his eyes felt like they were on fire, tears made his vision blurry, and his nose had started to run.

"Good job," Gryphon said, sliding the cutting board away from him and dumping the contents into the skillet on the stove.

Marina moved to his other side, placing a hand on his shoulder. A coolness spread up his neck from the point of contact to his face, taking away the sting in his eyes. He turned his head, catching a glimpse of an emerald green glow before it vanished when she removed her hand.

"What was—"

She gave him a soft smile and moved away without answering.

He blinked, then dabbed the moisture from his face with his sleeve. He hadn't imagined what he'd seen. And the significance rang in his head like a gong. Marina could produce an energy field just like

Libra, although it looked very different and had a different feel and effect.

Libra's field felt warm, energizing. And had revved him up like an engine. But Marina's had felt cool and soothing. And had taken away his discomfort.

Is that what brought this unusual family together? Were they all energy workers? If so, they were gifted beyond the scope most people even imagined possible. Were they living out here so they could practice and enhance their skills?

Regardless, he'd stumbled into nirvana. This was exactly the type of ability he'd wanted to study as part of his doctoral thesis, to prove the potential of the mind-body connection. He just hadn't known where to look to find his ideal candidates.

Now he did. He'd already considered asking Libra to work with him, kicking around potential ideas as he'd finished washing up the vegetables in the greenhouse. But having Marina as a second test case would be amazing. They had already achieved something he'd viewed as only theoretical. The potential inherent in that knowledge was staggering.

"You ready to tackle broccoli?"

Gryphon's question pulled him off his mental road trip. "Uh... yeah. Sure."

After Gryphon showed him how he wanted the dark green stalks cut, Brendan set to work. When he finished, he handed the cutting board to Gryphon.

He nodded with approval. "You're getting the hang of it. Now fetch the lemon-thyme pasta out of the cupboard." He pointed to one of the upper cupboards to the left of the sink.

Nothing inside the cupboard looked like it had been purchased in a store. Instead, the row upon row of neat containers, mostly glass, held a cornucopia of carefully preserved fruits and veggies, dried grains, and homemade pasta.

He pulled out the container labeled *lemon-thyme*, which held linguine-sized, pale yellow-cream pasta flecked with green. He held it up. "Did you make this?"

Gryphon glanced over his shoulder but kept stirring the broccoli and onions. "Yep. Never could get used to the pre-packaged stuff."

Was there anything Gryphon didn't source himself?

He handed him the container, watching as he dropped about a third of the contents into the large pot of boiling water on the stove. "Do you sell the pasta, too?"

"Not usually." Gryphon picked up a wooden spoon and started stirring. "It's a lot of work. I mostly do it for the family, and a few of our long-time customers." He motioned Brendan forward, handing him the wooden spoon. "Keep an eye on the pasta. It'll cook pretty well without interference, but you'll want to stir it every minute or two to keep it from clumping together."

"Okay."

While Gryphon moved about the kitchen, Marina and Lelindia set the table with the same precision his petite friend had shown at breakfast and lunch.

Which brought up another point. If Marina was an energy worker, there was a good chance Lelindia would have a talent for it, too. Had Marina tried teaching her yet? Would she be open to the idea if he suggested it? He had so many questions but didn't want to step on any toes now that he was gaining their trust.

At first, he'd thought their quiet existence was due to a lack of resources, a hurdle he could have helped them overcome. But he'd reevaluated that opinion, making a hundred-and-eighty-degree turn. For energy workers, this simple life would be ideal. They had everything they needed to create a nurturing environment that gave them the calm and peace to support their training.

He didn't want to do anything to upset that delicate balance. And he could, if he wasn't careful. His normal life was a far cry from simple. Right now he had an opportunity to take a short break from his fast-paced lifestyle, but eventually his responsibilities would call him back into the larger world.

Which presented a significant problem. If he wanted to see where his connection with Libra could lead, he'd have to convince her to join him in his world when he left.

Sixteen

By the time Libra finished the wreath, she'd calmed down considerably. Obsessing over the future of the Sahzade line was pointless when she and Brendan had known each other for less than a day. Yes, it had been an intense day, and she couldn't ignore the strength of their connection, but that didn't mean she had to decide tonight what she was going to do with the rest of her life.

Which made dinner a much more relaxed and enjoyable affair. Gryphon was back to his usual gregarious self, telling stories of their adventures since moving to the cabin.

Brendan sat to her left as he had at breakfast and lunch. Occasionally his knee would bump against hers, or the side of his hand would brush her arm, sending tingles along her skin. Those subtle touches reminded her of the delicious kiss they'd shared. And made her want to find a way to share another one before the evening ended.

Gryphon asked Brendan about his family, and he talked a bit about his parents, his love for them and their devotion to him coming through, as did their compassion for those suffering and in need. The stories he shared indicated his parents had regularly volunteered their time and expertise to provide assistance when natural disasters struck, both on Earth and on interstellar colonies.

His voice grew soft as he described the earthquake on New Athens that had killed them. But she didn't hear any regret, only sadness. It was clear his parents had lived full lives, and died doing something they believed in.

She respected and admired that. If it also made her feel guilty and homesick, well, that was her problem, not his.

"Thank you for another delicious meal, Gryphon," Brendan said as he rose from the table, picking up his plate and hers. "I'll take care of the dishes."

Gryphon smiled as he stood. "That would be great."

She saw an opportunity and took it. "I'll help."

Brendan met her gaze, the warm light in his eyes drawing her like a flame. "Thanks."

"Me, too!" Lelindia announced, sliding off her chair and hurrying into the kitchen to grab her stepstool.

Brendan chuckled as he watched her. "I don't think I was ever that eager to help with chores."

Marina stood, picking up Lelindia's plate and her own. "It's not the chore that's the draw, it's the man in charge of it. She's excited to have a new friend."

Brendan smiled, then gave Libra a wink. "That makes two of us."

More tingles, and not just on her arm.

She followed him into the kitchen, filling the sink with soapy water while he gathered the rest of the dishes and Lelindia positioned her stepstool next to the drying rack. Gryphon and Marina checked on the fire in the fireplace, then settled on the couch.

"I'll wash if you rinse," he said as he came up behind her, the nearness of his body putting her nerve endings on high alert.

She moved to the other side of the double sink. "Okay." Her voice squeaked slightly.

His smile told her he'd heard it. Or he might have been reading her emotional state. It wasn't like she could hide how he made her feel.

And those feelings intensified every time he handed her another dish and his fingers, arm, or body brushed against hers, which was quite frequently. She'd never considered washing dishes to be a sensual experience, but his presence completely changed the dynamic.

"I have a question for you," he said as he handed her one of the plates.

"Okay." She rinsed the plate and set it in the drying rack for Lelindia.

"Does the nearest town have any bars or restaurants that offer dancing on Saturday night?"

She paused, her hand partially open to accept the next plate. "Um, dancing?"

"Yeah." He met her gaze when she didn't take the plate. "You do like to dance, don't you?"

When he looked at her like that, she could barely remember her own name. "I don't know. I've never danced before."

He stared at her. "Never?"

She shook her head, dropping her gaze. If he kept spending time with her, he'd discover an entire universe of things she'd never done. And things she had that he'd never imagined in his wildest dreams.

He nudged her with his hip. "You up to giving it a try?"

His tone was playful, but his expression was serious.

She hesitated.

He bent closer. "I'd be honored to be your first dance partner."

Her gaze locked onto his full lips, and all resistance vanished. Dancing could easily lead to kissing. "Okay."

"Great! It's a date." His smile lit up the room.

Date. She'd never been on a date before, either. This day was full of surprises.

He held the plate out again. "I'll scout out the closest place and arrange transport for tomorrow night."

She took the plate, but almost forgot to rinse it before handing it to Lelindia, who had caught up with them while they talked.

"Can I go?" Lelindia asked, her expression hopeful.

"Not this time," Marina called out from the living room. Apparently she'd been listening in on their conversation.

Lelindia's smile faded.

Brendan picked up one of the water glasses. "But I can give you a lesson after we finish the dishes."

Her smile returned full force. "Okay!"

Libra smothered a laugh with her sleeve, pretending she was wiping water off her nose. This she had to see.

Brendan nudged her with his hip again, giving her a sidelong glance and a secret smile.

Oh, yes, she was going to enjoy this a lot.

After the chores were done, Marina and Gryphon helped them move the couch and chairs from in front of the fireplace, clearing a space on the floor for the dancing lesson.

Brendan helped Marina pick out a selection of suitable music on the media system built into the comm panel, before walking to the center of the room. He bowed low to Lelindia and offered his hand. "May I have this dance?"

"Yeah!" She practically leapt into his arms.

He caught her effortlessly, holding her steady as he guided her feet onto his. "To start, keep your feet on top of mine. That will help you get the rhythm."

She nodded vigorously, her dark hair bobbing.

Libra stood beside Marina and Gryphon as the music started. Brendan moved his feet in what looked like a squarish pattern.

"This is called a waltz," he said. "The basic pattern is a box, but you rotate it so you can move around the room." He kept up the gliding motion, carrying Lelindia with him as they circled the open space.

Lelindia giggled as her feet slipped, but Brendan kept hold of her, pausing so she could regain her position.

Libra kept close watch on Brendan's feet, memorizing the pattern as he moved, anticipating where it would carry him next. If Lelindia was dancing as an actual partner, rather than standing on his feet, she'd have to move in opposition, so that when he stepped forward, she stepped back.

By the time the song ended, Libra was impatient to give it a try. The amused look Brendan shot her made it clear he could feel her eagerness. He lifted Lelindia off his feet and set her on the floor. "Is it okay if I dance the next one with Libra?"

If Lelindia had adored him before, now she was looking at him with something approaching hero worship. "Uh-huh."

Libra knew the feeling, especially when Brendan focused his gaze on her. The tingles started up even before she took his hand and he led her to the center of the space. When his right hand circled her waist, she inhaled as mini explosions kicked off at every point of contact.

He brought his lips close to her ear as he captured her right hand in his left. "Will your field engage?" he whispered.

She hadn't even considered that possibility. But the way she felt right now, it just might. "I don't know," she whispered back.

"Guess we'll find out. Put your left hand on my shoulder."

She did as he instructed, feeling his muscles flex beneath her fingers. Oh, yeah, her field could definitely engage if she didn't work to stop it.

Brendan nodded at Marina. "All set."

The music started, a different tune but with a similar rhythm.

"Think you've got the pattern?" he asked her.

She nodded.

"Then follow me."

The easy pressure on her hand and waist told her exactly how he wanted her to move, but she wasn't even sure that mattered. From the moment he took the first step, she felt like they were moving as one, completely in sync, floating through the pattern effortlessly.

Surprise lit his beautiful eyes, followed by a growing awareness that stole air from her lungs. The pressure of his hand on her lower back increased a fraction as he urged her closer.

She went willingly. Hopefully he was watching where they were going, because she sure wasn't. All she could see, all she could sense, all she knew was him.

His gaze dropped to her mouth, and he licked his lips.

Warmth flowed through her, but he gave a little shake of his head, like he was coming out of a daydream, and looked into her eyes.

The banked fire she saw there sent an answering flare of heat to her core. The tremor of her energy field rising to the surface brought her back to reality. She reined it in as they continued to circle the floor. She didn't want to get into a discussion about it tonight and possibly ruin the mood.

When the music ended he stilled, holding her gaze as his palm caressed her back. "Thank you for a lovely dance."

"Thank you for my first dance."

He nodded, the look in his eyes promising a cornucopia of firsts still to come.

She couldn't wait.

Seventeen

Dancing with Libra had been heaven and hell all in one. He'd never dreamed he'd experience the kind of seamless flowing beauty they'd shared. It had felt like they'd been dancing together all their lives.

But they'd also had an audience. He'd had to fight to keep that in mind every second he'd held her in his arms. When the music had ended, he'd wanted to kiss her lush lips and let go of rational thought. But he'd held onto reason, barely, returning his focus to Lelindia for the remainder of the evening.

He'd hoped to end the night with a goodnight kiss, but even that hadn't been possible with Gryphon and Marina acting as chaperones. He'd wondered if Libra would come out to the living room after they'd gone to bed, but she didn't.

Now he was lying on the couch, staring up at the beamed ceiling in the soft glow from the nightlight in the kitchen. He'd managed to fall asleep after he'd given up on a visit from Libra, but chaotic dreams and the brush of her emotions had woken him early.

She was awake, too. He could feel it. And thinking about him, based on the tenor of her emotions. Maybe even wishing he was in her bed, although she didn't seem inclined to do anything about it.

Which confused the heck out of him. He'd never met a more sensual, responsive woman. Or a more guarded one. And yet, in many ways she seemed innocent, naïve even. How was that possible? How could both sets of facts be true?

One thing was certain. He wanted to learn everything he could about Libra Hawke. In less than twenty-four hours, she'd become essential in a way he couldn't define. It was illogical, irrational, and completely out of character for him. He made friends easily, but because of his empathic abilities, deeper relationships were rare, and usually developed over months or even years.

Libra had skipped right over all his usual checkpoints, burrowing into his heart from the first moment he'd seen her. Her energy abilities made her incredibly special, which might explain his instant attraction, but there was a lot more to their connection than that. And to her story.

The click of the bathroom door closing brought him out of his musings. Someone else was awake. A quick check of the emotional fields in the cabin told him it was Gryphon.

Pushing the thick blankets aside, he stood and padded over to his suitcases to fetch a change of clothes. He had the bundle in his hands when Gryphon walked into the living room, stifling a yawn.

"Morning," Gryphon said, running his hand through his hair and heading for the kitchen.

"Morning." Brendan held up the bundle. "I was going to take a quick shower if that's okay."

Gryphon nodded. "Sure, sure."

The warm water didn't help to suppress his thoughts of Libra, but it made him feel more human. By the time he exited the bathroom, clean and ready to tackle the day, the scent of coffee had filled the hallway, drifting down from the kitchen. He tucked his dirty clothes in a bag in his suitcase, then joined Gryphon in the kitchen.

"Coffee?" Gryphon asked, holding up the pot.

"Thanks." He snagged a mug from the cupboard and held it while Gryphon poured. "Smells good."

"It should. Comes from a local roaster. We get a fresh batch every weekend."

That fit in with everything else he'd observed about their lifestyle. And the coffee tasted as good as it smelled.

Marina strolled into the living room, her dark hair pulled up into a thick ponytail. She gave him a warm smile. "I see you're a morning person."

He held up the full mug. "I am when good coffee's brewing." He looked to see if Libra or Lelindia were with her. No sign of either.

"Lelindia's still sleeping," Marina said, following the direction of his gaze. "And Libra's in the shower."

In the shower? Had she snuck down the hall as soon as he'd joined Gryphon in the kitchen?

The timing was suspicious. He should have passed her in the hallway or seen her leave her room while he was putting away his clothes in the living room. But she'd waited until he was in the kitchen to make her move. Having Libra avoiding him was not the way he'd wanted to start the day.

Gryphon poured a mug of coffee for Marina and then turned to Brendan. "Breakfast on market days is a feed yourself affair. We've got plenty of fruit, bread, nut butters, and jams to choose from. We have eggs, too, but since you don't cook..." He shrugged.

Brendan waved a hand. "No problem. I can manage just fine."

"Good." Gryphon started fixing a plate for himself. "What time are they coming to fetch your plane?"

"Not sure yet, but I expect nine-thirty at the latest."

Gryphon nodded. "Well, we can leave you a key to the cabin. You'll have the place to yourself until we get back this afternoon."

That gave him pause. He hadn't stopped to think that logically he'd be alone in their house for several hours. Or that Gryphon's attitude would have altered so dramatically that he'd be okay with that. A lot had changed in the past twenty-four hours. "Thank you. I appreciate it."

Gryphon nodded again, a teasing light in his eyes. "We'll have lunch when we get back. Don't try to cook anything."

Brendan grinned. "Don't worry, I won't." But that begged the question of what he would do.

Ordinarily he'd be caught up in the normal flow of his life, answering messages, dealing with company matters, and studying. But other than checking out the restaurant situation for his date with

Libra and confirming the flatbed's arrival time with Mary Kay, he didn't have anything else needing his attention. "I'll have some time on my hands. Do you have any chores you need done?"

Gryphon and Marina exchanged an unusually long glance.

He'd known some couples who had excellent non-verbal communication skills, and maybe that's what he was seeing, but it felt more like a full-blown conversation without words.

"The fireplace is due to be swept out," Marina finally said, turning to him. "Normally that's Libra's job, but I'm sure she'd be willing to turn it over to you for today."

The mention of Libra's name made him want to purr like a cat. "Great." He'd never cleaned a fireplace before, but how hard could it be?

"I'll have her show you what to do as soon as she's out of the shower."

That image made him want to do more than purr. *Stay focused.* "Thanks. I'll have it shipshape by this afternoon."

Marina's small smile, and the laughter he could feel her suppressing, made it clear he wasn't fooling her. She knew exactly where his thoughts had taken him.

By the time Libra put in an appearance, Marina had claimed the shower and Gryphon was rousing Lelindia. Brendan had already finished his breakfast and was washing his dishes. He'd discovered that the kitchen had a dishwasher with a wood panel front that blended with the rustic decor, but the family didn't seem to use it for daily dishes, so he hadn't either. *When in Rome.*

Libra walked into the kitchen looking like a woodland sprite, her damp hair pulled into a topknot, a few strands curling around the base. Her color was high, and her rosy lips tempted him to claim a kiss. She gave him a sidelong glance as she made a beeline for the refrigerator, head down as though he wouldn't see her if she moved quickly enough.

He smiled, projecting his joy at her. "Good morning, Libra."

She paused, turning partially to face him, the flush on her cheeks growing more pronounced. "Good morning, Brendan."

Without his empathic abilities, he might have mistaken that flush for embarrassment. But the warm flow of desire that enveloped him told him the truth. She wasn't avoiding looking at him because she was feeling shy or embarrassed. She was avoiding him because looking at him was flipping her switches.

And wasn't that the nicest good morning he'd ever had.

He leaned back against the counter, folding his arms over his chest. It was a shameless ploy. He knew the pose would emphasize the muscle definition in his arms and chest, visible under his long-sleeved T-shirt. But he couldn't resist, not with the glow in her eyes turning up his internal thermostat. "Sleep well?"

She coughed. "Um, yes." Her gaze moved over him in an unconscious appraisal that had a predictable effect on his nether regions.

Thank goodness for the concealing power of thick denim.

Her gaze met his. What he saw made the denim start to pinch.

"Did you?"

He frowned, not following. "Did I what?"

The corner of her mouth twitched, and her voice dropped to a throaty whisper. "Did you sleep well?"

"Uh…" Words failed him. His petite sprite had turned the tables on him, going from nymph to seductress in the blink of an eye. She sauntered toward him, the sway of her hips making him think of things he needed to stop thinking about.

She halted a hand's breadth away. "I dreamt about you."

Not helping. He pressed his biceps against his hands to keep from reaching for her. "Did you?" His voice was almost an octave too high.

"Mm-hmm." Lifting her hand, she used one finger to lightly trace the curve of his upper arm.

He clenched his jaw to suppress the tremors her touch triggered.

"It was a lovely dream." She tilted her head up, the tip of her tongue brushing over her lips. "But I think reality will be even better."

Game over. Brendan zero, Libra one thousand sixty-two.

With a groan, he bent down, claiming the kiss he'd been denied last night.

Eighteen

Libra hadn't set out to seduce Brendan. Far from it.

She'd spent most of the night trying to keep her emotions — and libido — under wraps, with varying degrees of success. Her dreams had been filled with passionate kisses and the rich caress of his voice. Whenever she awoke, which was often, her internal tracking system kept reminded her of just *how close* he was. Only a wall separated them. More than once she'd seriously considered joining him in the living room or drawing him into the privacy of her bedroom.

But sanity had prevailed.

Unfortunately, her body hadn't thanked her for it. By the time Brendan had started moving around this morning, she'd been aching for his touch. Which is why she'd stayed in her room. But then he'd taken a shower. Another hurdle. Picturing him naked, water running over his skin, had almost put her out of her mind, especially because she was fighting to keep her emotions from telegraphing to him.

As soon as he'd moved into the kitchen, she'd taken the coldest shower of her life and focused on what she needed to do to get ready for the market. That had worked until she'd seen him standing at the kitchen sink, looking far too at home in the simple setting, his muscles moving beneath his snug shirt, his hair still damp from his shower.

Just like that, she'd lost all the ground she'd gained, her body dragging her forward like a magnet.

She'd resisted by heading straight to the refrigerator.

And then he'd said her name.

That had stopped her forward momentum. And when she'd gotten a full view of him leaning against the counter, the look in his eyes beckoning her, her inner vixen had come out to play.

His response had turned up the heat. She'd wanted to know if she could break through his self-control.

Now she had her answer.

The contact with his warm mouth sent shockwaves through her body. She rose onto tiptoe and sank her fingers into his damp hair, but he kept his arms folded, his body still. Maybe he didn't trust himself to not lose track of their surroundings if he pulled her closer.

She respected the line he'd drawn. And the respect he was showing her.

Instead of pushing the limits, she reveled in the sensual delight of a kiss that tempted, teased, and promised without any pressure to turn it into something more.

By the time she released him, he was smiling, his blue eyes sparkling.

"I could get used to that kind of greeting," he murmured.

"So could I." At that moment, she couldn't imagine how she'd lived all her life without this.

He brushed his lips briefly over hers before pushing away from the counter, backing her up in the process. "Marina said you could show me how to clean out the fireplace."

That was an odd segue. "Why?"

Laughter danced in his eyes. "Because I'm going to need something to keep me occupied while you're at the market. Manual labor seemed like a good idea."

Now she understood. He'd had as frustrating a night as she had and needed a way to release some of that tension. She knew of a more enjoyable solution, but it wasn't practical in their current situation. "Okay. Follow me."

Walking him through her cleaning routine didn't take long. By the time they were finished, Lelindia had joined them, her typical low-grade morning energy level ramping up now that she was in the presence of her new friend.

Libra grabbed a quick breakfast while Lelindia kept Brendan occupied. Marina and Gryphon joined them not long after, and together they loaded the last of the market items in the transport.

Gryphon held a key out to Brendan. "If you need anything, the number for the market's customer service booth is coded into the comm panel. You can reach us through them."

Brendan accepted the key. "Good to know. Anything else I can do for you while you're gone?"

Gryphon grinned. "You any good at cleaning toilets, boy?"

Marina snorted and Libra ducked her head to hide a smile. Gryphon hated cleaning the bathroom, partly because his height made the compact space uncomfortable for crouching.

Brendan didn't bat an eye. "You bet. Any man worth his salt can clean a bathroom and a window, old man."

Gryphon's teasing grin turned into a full-fledged smile. "Then by all means, have at it."

Brendan nodded. "I will." He turned to her. "And I'll make all the arrangements for tonight."

Tonight. Their date. "I'm looking forward to it."

His smile made her tummy dance. "Me, too."

Brendan stood on the front stoop, waving as they drove away. She waved back and watched him through the trees until the cabin was out of sight.

Leaving him behind felt strange. How had he become so integrated into her life in the space of a day? Everything about this situation had a feeling of unreality. How they'd met. His ability to see her field. Their connection when they'd kissed.

He was Human, she was Suulh. They were from two different worlds. Literally.

And yet, she'd never felt more grounded, more sure of herself, than she did right now. When she was with Brendan, her fears and anxieties receded, joy and hope taking their place. Being with him was like standing in the warmth of the sun, surrounded by the rich colors of a world filled with beauty and light. She hadn't felt anything remotely like it since...

A wall slammed up, blocking out the memories on the other side.

That was the past. She couldn't change it. Couldn't bring it back. And couldn't fix it, no matter how much she wanted to. No point in thinking about it.

"I can't believe you asked him to clean the bathroom," Marina said, giving Gryphon a mock-stern glance. "He's a guest, not a cleaning service."

Gryphon shrugged. "He offered. And we're providing room and board. Seemed like a fair trade to me."

"And so convenient, since this happens to be your week to clean the bathroom."

"Is it?" His brows lifted. "I hadn't realized that."

Marina rolled her eyes, her gaze meeting Libra's. He wasn't fooling either of them. Over the years, he'd tried all manner of bribes and trades to get out of that particular chore, usually without success.

But he'd found a willing cohort in Brendan.

"Besides, he's cleaning the fireplace, too. That's Libra's job."

She couldn't let that go unchallenged. "The difference is, I *like* cleaning the fireplace." It was her favorite part of the cabin. And in the summer months when they didn't use it, she'd set up mini light displays with seasonal decorations in the space so it was always festive and cheerful. "I'm also not the one who talked him into doing it."

Another shrug. "I didn't talk him into anything. He asked me. He was looking for work. Do you want him sitting around for hours, bored and alone?"

"No, but–"

"But nothing. Tomorrow we can bring him with us. Today, he's helping with chores. Everybody wins. And you and I can help Marina with her tasks so it's all balanced."

Marina folded her arms. "You're very pleased with yourself, aren't you?"

Gryphon grinned, all pretense cast aside. "Yes, I am."

Nineteen

Loading Romeo onto the flatbed took a chunk of the morning, but his plane was now headed to Far Horizon's maintenance hangar outside Palm Springs where work would begin on repairs and restoration.

When Brendan returned to the cabin, he used the comm panel to contact Mary Kay.

"Romeo's on his way." He gave her a quick rundown.

"I'll head over to the hangar to check their progress in a few days."

"Thank you." The trip wasn't necessary. His work crews were the best in the business. But Mary Kay was almost as fond of Romeo as he was. The plane had been a part of his family's story for a long time.

"And how are you?" she asked, her voice dropping into the maternal tone he knew so well.

That was a much happier topic. "Great! Loving being in the woods and slowing things down a bit."

"Everything's going well with the people you're staying with?"

A memory of that morning's kiss with Libra sent a trail of heat through his body. "Yep." And tonight he'd have her all to himself for a few hours. He couldn't wait.

"Do you need me to ship anything to you?"

"No, I'm good for now." He'd expected to be hiking the mountain trails on Gaia during his vacation, so the wardrobe he'd packed for that would work just as well for an extended cabin stay. "But you'll be getting a package from me of the best dark chocolate brownies you've ever tasted."

After confirming with Gryphon that they could be safely shipped, he'd paid him for a dozen plus shipping to send a box by express delivery while the family was in town this morning.

She laughed. "Oh, dear. You know my weakness."

"I should hope so. You were the one who always brought chocolate treats to work when you knew I'd be there."

"Of course! Your parents had to set boundaries, but I got to spoil you all I wanted. And now I'm reaping the benefits."

He grinned. Spoiling Mary Kay was one of his favorite things in life. She'd been his lifeline after his parents had died. Talking to her always made them feel closer. "Well, if you enjoy them as much as I think you will, I'll have Gryphon send out another package the next time he makes a batch."

"Are you trying to expand my waistline?"

He chuckled. "That's not possible and you know it." Mary Kay was the most fit sixty-something woman he knew. She used a bike to get around whenever she was working at the shipyards or the extensive warehouses of the R&D department, and biked a minimum of twenty miles a day when she was at home.

"Well, thank you for the gift. I'm sure I'll love them."

He glanced at the clock. "And I'd better get going. I have some chores to tackle."

"Chores? I thought you were lounging around by a warm fire."

"Not when there's work to be done. Gotta earn my keep."

He could hear the smile in her voice. "Then I'll let you get to it. Alert me if you need anything."

"Will do."

After he ended the call, he checked the local restaurant listings and located one called Redwoods that had an attached bar area offering live music and dancing on Fridays and Saturdays. Perfect. He scheduled a transport to arrive at the cabin at six.

With his plans settled, he focused on the fireplace cleanup. Gryphon had been teasing when he'd asked him if he wanted to clean the bathroom, but he was all for pitching in. He'd never had a reason to learn how to cook, but his parents had been adamant about the necessity for leaving any place where he stayed in better condition than he'd found it. He'd cleaned his own bathroom since the age of seven. The only reason he hired a cleaning service at his house now was because he was rarely there for longer than a few days at a time.

Sweeping out the fireplace naturally led to thoughts of last night's dancing lesson. He couldn't remember the last time he'd had so much fun. Lelindia was adorable, and so earnest, exactly the kind of kid he'd love to have someday. He'd never given the idea of fatherhood much thought until now, mostly because he'd never found the right woman. Spending time with Lelindia had given that idea form, and the vague outlines had crystalized into a solid image when Libra had moved into his arms. The feeling of connection as he'd held her close had captured him in bonds he didn't want to break. Ever.

Tonight, he'd get to enjoy that feeling again, and for more than a single song.

The direction of his daydreams ended up heating him more than the physical labor. By the time he moved on to the bathroom, he welcomed the cool water as he scrubbed and rinsed the shower before tackling the toilet and sink. A check of the time confirmed he still had at least half an hour on his own, so he scrubbed the kitchen sink and wiped down the counters.

He'd noted when he'd started that all the cleaning products in the house were homemade, just like the food. He'd found dark glass bottles of what he assumed were essential oils in one of the kitchen cupboards, each one neatly labeled. The spray he was using in the kitchen smelled like a citrus grove, clean and invigorating.

He was sweeping the floor when he heard the tromp of footsteps on the walkway.

"We're home!" Gryphon's voice boomed out as he swung the front door wide.

Lelindia raced past him, spotted Brendan in the kitchen, and charged forward, smacking into him and wrapping her small arms around his legs.

He wobbled slightly, using the broom for extra stability. "Hi."

She beamed up at him but didn't let go. "Hi!"

He caught the flickers of amusement from the others as they watched his reaction to Lelindia's enthusiastic greeting. "Did you have fun at the market?"

Her head bobbed, her ponytail swinging. "We sold *lots* of stuff!"

"Glad to hear it." He glanced at Libra, who'd moved next to the barstools. "Hi."

"Hi." Her outward reaction to seeing him wasn't nearly as unfettered as Lelindia's, but the emotions he sensed underneath the calm façade were every bit as joyful. She surveyed the kitchen and fireplace. "You've been busy."

"He sure has," Gryphon agreed as he carried a couple canvas bags into the kitchen and set them on the counter. "We should leave you alone more often, boy."

Brendan grinned. "Anytime, old man."

Gryphon chuckled. "You about ready for lunch?"

"Starving."

"Then I'll warm up the stew from yesterday. It's even better after it's marinated for a day."

"Sounds good." He extricated himself from Lelindia's grip and returned the broom to the laundry room with the other cleaning supplies.

Libra was waiting for him when he stepped into the hallway. "Hi," she whispered, resting her palms on his chest and brushing a quick kiss across his lips.

The brief contact made his breath catch. "Hi," he whispered back, returning the kiss with a slightly longer one of his own. But when her fingers curled into the fabric of his shirt, he pulled back. She tempted him far too much to give into his impulses now. "So, things went well at the market?"

She nodded. "We'll need to gather more vegetables this afternoon to take tomorrow."

More time in the greenhouse with her? Sounded delightful. Dangerous, but delightful. "I'm happy to help."

She gave him a look that made it clear she knew exactly what he was thinking. "Marina and Lelindia will be working with us."

"Oh."

Now she was trying to hold in a laugh. He must have telegraphed his disappointment more than he'd thought.

"But we could take a walk afterward."

Much more promising. "I'd love to."

"Good." She nodded toward the bathroom door behind him. "Did you end up cleaning the bathroom?"

He smiled. "Yep."

"Really?"

"Did you think I wouldn't?"

"I don't know. Gryphon hates that chore."

"Well, I don't. Cleaning is satisfying work." And the look of respect in her eyes didn't hurt, either.

She studied him, her head tilting slightly, making her look impish. "You're an unusual Human."

Human?

She blinked as a jolt of anxiety darted through her emotional field. "I mean man. Human man. Male." The faster she talked, the more flustered she became, her body tightening up like a bow.

He rested his hands on her shoulders, applying gentle pressure to calm her down. "Is that a good thing?"

She met his gaze, her body stilling under his touch. "I think so."

He gave her a soft smile. "Good, because your opinion means a lot to me."

Her muscles grew pliable under his hands as her anxiety ebbed away. Her gaze traced the contours of his face, finally settling on his mouth. "Are we going dancing tonight?"

The throaty question almost undid his good intentions. "Yes. The transport's picking us up at six."

She nodded without taking her gaze off his lips. "Good." She leaned forward.

"'Scuse me!"

They jerked apart as Lelindia skipped down the hallway.

"Gotta use the bathroom."

He stepped aside and bowed slightly, gesturing to the open bathroom door. "All clean and ready for you, milady."

Lelindia paused, giving him a quizzical look.

Maybe she'd never heard the term before. "Milady is a form of address for a woman of noble birth. For royalty."

Lelindia beamed. "Like Nedale!"

The blast of cold fear from Libra caught him off guard. He turned and found the color had drained from her cheeks.

She didn't look at him, focusing instead on Lelindia. "After you wash up, I'll help you set the table."

Lelindia looked between them, clearly confused, but she gave a child's carefree shrug and skipped into the bathroom, closing the door behind her.

Libra started to turn away, but he caught her arm. "What's wrong?"

She kept her gaze on the floor. "Nothing."

"Libra." He cradled her jaw, urging her to face him. "Empath, remember? You were terrified." And she still was. Even without his empathic senses, he'd be able to feel the tremors in her body. "What is it? What scared you?"

She took a few slow breaths, struggling to regain her composure. "I can't tell you."

"Can't? Or won't?"

She didn't answer him, but anxiety had joined the fear swirling around her.

The combination tore at him, especially since he suspected he was the cause. And he had no idea why.

He said the only thing he could, repeating what he'd told her the day before. "Whatever you're holding back, you don't need to fear me. I would never hurt you."

The turmoil he saw in her blue eyes almost brought tears to his. "Never," she murmured, like the word was unfamiliar.

"Never," he repeated firmly, his thumb brushing her cheek.

He had to make her understand, had to get past the barrier she'd thrown up between them like a forcefield.

She was terrified of something, but he wasn't convinced it was him, specifically. More like what he represented. Which meant even if she trusted him, as she claimed she did, the fear would always hold sway, pushing between them.

He had to help her work through it, conquer it. Had to let her know she wasn't alone in this fight.

He'd planned to be her guide during her emotional journey. But he was also prepared to be her champion. "And I promise you this." He drew her closer, circling his arm protectively around her shoulders. "I will never allow anyone else to hurt you, either."

Twenty

Libra's mind and body were at war.

The core of her being, her physical and energetic essence, accepted Brendan's words without question, without doubt, without fear.

But her mind poked holes in that certainty, tearing it apart.

He was Human. A stranger she'd known for a day. And he was asking her to trust him with a secret that had the power to destroy her life, and the lives of everyone she loved.

She couldn't do it. Couldn't make that leap, at least not yet. If he knew the truth about her, about them, his attitude could change. He could reject her. Or worse, expose her, forcing her to run from the first place that had felt like home since she was a child.

She had to hold onto her secret until she was certain he could handle it.

But seeing the pain in his eyes made her heart weep.

"Do you believe me?" he finally asked, his voice strained.

How could she answer that question? "I want to." That, at least, was the complete truth.

Another flash of pain flickered across his face. His lips pressed together, but he nodded. "That's a start."

The bathroom door opened behind him.

He released her, stepping back as Lelindia pranced toward them. "I should probably wash up, too."

It seemed like a convenient excuse to give her some space.

She'd take it. "Okay." Turning, she followed Lelindia down the hall to the living room.

The familiar scent of warm bread and stew helped to ground her, as did watching Marina and Gryphon moving about the kitchen in perfect harmony. This was what she was protecting, what she stood to lose if she revealed too much to Brendan too quickly. She'd lost so much already. She wasn't willing to risk destroying the life they'd carved out in this little nook of the galaxy.

Pulling her shoulders back, she marched into the kitchen and took dishes and silverware out of the cupboards. By the time Brendan appeared, she had her emotions firmly in hand. No matter what happened between them, she had to think of her family first. He'd either have to accept that or... move on.

The thought made her gut clench, but she ignored it. If she was the one making all the rules, she couldn't complain if he chose not to play the game.

Marina shot her looks throughout lunch, and Brendan didn't try to touch her once. Gryphon read the room well. He kept up a lively patter of conversation with Lelindia, the two of them sharing stories with Brendan about the people they'd seen at the market, filling what would likely have been an uncomfortable silence.

Brendan smiled and laughed at all the appropriate places, but he was more subdued than she'd ever seen him. Which proved her point. If one awkward conversation could change his behavior, she needed to tread cautiously.

After lunch, Gryphon stayed for clean-up duty while she and Brendan followed Marina and Lelindia to the greenhouse.

Brendan was quiet. He didn't try to take her hand, either.

She snuck peeks at him as they walked down the trail. What she saw wasn't encouraging. His mouth was turned down and lines furrowed his forehead.

About halfway down the path, he let out a deep sigh, turning to look at her. The sadness she saw in his eyes brought her to a halt.

"Libra, do you want me to leave?" The words came out thick, ponderous.

Her chest tightened. Leave? *Now?* "No!"

She hadn't meant to put so much force behind the word. He stumbled back like she'd shoved him. She also realized Marina had halted farther up the path, pivoting to face them.

She waved to her. "Go ahead. We'll be right there."

Marina gave a slow nod, her gaze moving between them before she turned and walked on.

Libra focused on Brendan, who was watching her like she was an injured bird he wanted to help but was afraid to touch.

She fixed the problem by placing her hand over his heart. "I don't want you to leave." Her energy field danced under her palm, but she held it in check. "Not unless that's what you want."

The guarded look fell away. "I want to be with you."

His words acted like a caress, stroking her nerve endings and pulling at her energy field.

"But it feels like my presence is causing you pain and triggering fear."

He wasn't wrong. But he wasn't right, either. Fear was her ever-present companion, not a stranger he'd brought into her home. And pain had camped out in her heart since she was a child. "Those aren't the only feelings you're triggering." She allowed her energy field to flow outward, wrapping around his body and hers, drawing them into a nurturing cocoon.

His breath caught, his gaze moving over the pearlescent glow. He lifted a hand, studying the shifting energy as it passed along his skin. "Your mental discipline is extraordinary."

She shrugged off the compliment. It was hard to take credit for something she'd been able to do since she was an infant.

Her shielding was another story. That took effort to maintain, especially if she had to expand it to protect more than herself. "I've had a lot of practice." Mostly as a child on Feylahn. Marina had insisted on keeping up her training after they'd settled on Gaia, and again here, but their sessions were a far cry from the strenuous lessons she remembered when she'd been working with her mother and Breaa, Marina's mother. She also had little cause to use her shield since moving here. Marina and Lelindia could heal any injury they sustained, and Gryphon was always with one of them. They didn't need physical protection. Her ability had become superfluous.

Except when a plane comes bearing down on you.

Well, yes, there was that. But what had protected her had injured Brendan. She still had nagging guilt about that.

"How old were you when you started?"

"Started what?"

"Practicing your energy abilities."

"Hard to say. When I was little, I thought of it as playing games. I didn't realize I was in training until I got older."

His gaze sharpened, but he asked his next question with a feather touch. "You learned from your parents, didn't you?"

An image of her mother floated through her mind, carrying the echo of remembered pain and sadness. "Yes."

"No wonder it means so much to you."

She nodded, not trusting herself to speak.

He placed his hand over hers. "When my parents died, I grieved for a long time. But I also learned that those we've lost never truly leave us. They're always in here." He pressed her hand against his heart.

Moisture gathered at the back of her eyes.

He curled his fingers around hers, his gaze intent. "You're in my heart, too."

Her lips parted, her pulse fluttering.

"I know it's crazy to say it. Maybe even crazy to think it. Two days ago, I didn't even know you existed. But I want to be completely open with you about how I feel. Crazy or not, I'm falling in love with you."

Her heart thumped in her chest so hard she wondered if it would crack a rib. "You're falling in love with me?"

"Yes. Which is why when I feel your pain, your fear, I want to do something to help you. But I can't if I'm the cause, and I don't understand why."

They were back to the discussion in the hallway, when Lelindia's offhand comment had driven an ice pick of fear between her shoulder blades.

He took a step closer, cradling her hand in both of his. "I know you have secrets, Libra. And I'm not asking you to share them, not until you're ready. Or not at all," he quickly added.

He must have sensed the flash of anxiety he'd sparked.

"I'm just asking you to be honest about how you feel. Hiding from your emotions won't work with me."

And that was the rub, wasn't it? She'd spent most of her life hiding from her emotions, stuffing them away, along with all the memories and knowledge of her past that had become more explosive than a supernova.

"I know you're confused," he continued. "And scared. And worried. I feel it all. But I also know you care about me as much as I care about you." His blue eyes looked like sunlight on the ocean, warming her from the inside out. "Our unusual connection is probably what's making all this rise to the surface."

He seemed to understand her better than she understood herself. The pull of their connection drew her closer. "I never expected you."

"I never expected you, either. But I'm very glad we found each other."

His smile focused all her attention on his mouth. "Me, too." She rose up as he bent down.

Contact! The brush of his lips made her energy field flare, changing it from a warm blanket to a smoldering ember.

He groaned, sealing their lips together for a searing kiss before breaking the connection and stepping back, putting distance between their bodies. "You have no idea how hard it is to stay sane when you do that." He took a shaky breath, his gaze shifting to the greenhouse. "But I'm not going to get you in trouble with Marina and Gryphon."

She choked back a laugh. "You wouldn't." Apparently, even with his empathic senses, he hadn't picked up on the fact that she was the final authority of the group. Not surprising, perhaps. She rarely exerted that authority. But she had after the accident. She'd insisted they bring him back to the cabin and put him in her bed.

She hadn't been able to explain why at the time, but she'd overridden Gryphon's objections, even as her heart had pounded with fear. Her subconscious must have picked up on the instant connection her conscious mind couldn't fathom.

He squeezed her hand, entwining their fingers and tugging her toward the greenhouse. "I also don't want to shirk my duties."

Neither did she, although looking at him gave her a heck of a good reason to do just that.

Twenty-One

Lelindia had stationed herself at the wash rack rather than helping her mother gather the vegetables. The hopeful look she'd given Brendan when he'd entered the greenhouse with Libra had made him smile.

While Libra and Marina brought them items to be cleaned, he worked beside and talked with his young friend. She knew almost as much about the plants they were washing, and the ones in the nearby trays, as Libra did, although she had issues pronouncing some of the terms. Whatever she said that he couldn't understand, he figured out through context or her emotional cues.

Which didn't even require the use of his empathic skills. She was the most artless child he'd ever met. Whatever she felt or thought she expressed, without any guile or hesitation. By the time they were ready to leave the greenhouse, he knew she thought he was beautiful, strong, funny, and smart. She'd also informed him that she loved him as much as brownies, which was a whole lot.

He'd managed to match her serious expression when he'd replied to that, even though inside he'd been grinning like a little kid. Her stamp of approval warmed his heart. And he'd assured her he loved her as much as brownies, too. How could he not?

After they'd loaded the bins of produce into the transport, Marina and Lelindia had headed into the cabin while Libra had clasped his hand in hers, pulling him onto the narrow path he'd walked to reach Romeo. But rather than heading west past the cabin, she took a different branch going south toward the nearby creek.

"This is my favorite path," she told him as the gurgle of the water grew louder. "It goes through some of the oldest growth in this section of the forest."

The crisp air was filled with the chatter of birds and the whisper of the wind in the trees. "It's very peaceful."

She nodded, her eyes closing for a moment as she inhaled deeply. "It's so full of life." Her gaze met his. "So are you."

"Thank you." No one had ever described him that way before. But he'd also never met anyone who engaged with the physical world the way Libra did. She seemed to be sensing the life around her in much the same way he sensed emotions. And since she'd learned to control her energetic field, she might also be able to interact with the energy fields of other living things in ways he could only imagine.

They came to a small stone and wood footbridge that crossed the creek, the path continuing on the other side. She paused at the center of the bridge, gazing at the water rippling over the rocks. "I could stand here for hours."

He doubted she was exaggerating. "Do you ever go in the water? Or is it too cold?"

"It's cold, especially this time of year." Her eyes sparkled as much as the winding creek. "But we've never let that stop us."

He could stand here and gaze at her for hours, too. "Want to go in now?" He wasn't nearly as nonchalant about near-freezing water as she seemed to be. He preferred the milder ocean temperatures of Hawaii's beaches. But he'd gladly go along with anything that would keep her lit up like she was now.

She smiled, like she knew he wasn't as eager as he'd tried to appear. "Not today."

Giving him a soft tug, she crossed over the bridge to the far side and continued along the path.

The forest surrounded them on all sides, making it easy to pretend they were the only two people under the canopy of branches. "How many other homes are in the area?"

"Two besides ours. From what our landlord told us when we moved in, most people sold back the land for reforestation long ago, rather than choosing to abide by the restrictions of living within the forest's expanded boundaries. Our lease agreement stipulates exactly how we have to manage the surrounding woods, and what types of potential issues we're expected to monitor and report to the forest service. An inspector also comes out twice a year to make sure everything is being handled according to the guidelines."

"Have you had any problems following the guidelines?"

She gave him a strange look. "Why would we?"

He opened his mouth, then closed it. Why, indeed? Their simple, earthy lifestyle would fit into the paradigm she'd described perfectly.

They walked in companionable silence for a while, the crunch of leaves and pebbles under their feet adding to the sigh of the breeze. The pace Libra set kept him plenty warm, as did the delightful feeling of her hand snugly tucked into his. She gave him occasional sidelong glances, and the deeper they moved into the woods, the more he could feel her growing excitement and sense of anticipation.

"Are we going somewhere specific?" he asked.

"One of my favorite picnic spots."

That sounded like fun. "Too bad I didn't think to snag some of Gryphon's treats before we left."

"We won't need them." The look that followed her comment knocked all thought of chocolate from his mind.

His grip on her hand tightened as his body reacted. "We won't?"

She shook her head.

"How—" The croak he produced resembled a bullfrog's. Swallowing, he tried again. "How much farther?" *Please, let it be close.*

Her smile made his knees move in funny ways. "Not far."

He couldn't manage any more conversation after that. Whatever she had planned, he was all in.

A large object loomed over the path up ahead. A fallen tree, one of the ancient giants that had once stood watch over the forest. It looked peaceful, lying in quiet repose amongst its much smaller offspring. He could see the base sloping skyward to their left, the massive trunk and remains of gnarled roots creating a natural pyramid effect, at least from this angle.

The path didn't go around the slumbering giant, it went underneath it. The wide base prevented the trunk from lying flat on the ground, creating an angled tunnel. Minor cuts into the surrounding bark had opened the gap to provide clearance to easily walk underneath.

He hadn't realized he'd stopped to stare until Libra spoke. "Come say hello."

Say hello?

He followed her as she moved off the path to the point where the tree rested flush on the ground. She placed her palm on the rough bark, her energy field engaging, the glow pulsing at the point of contact.

He watched her, fascinated by her emotional reaction. She seemed to be drawing strength from the tree, as though its solid bulk somehow gave her power. And while the sensations were difficult to define, it felt like a mutually beneficial energetic interaction. "Is the tree still alive?" He couldn't imagine how that was possible, but he was learning to keep a very open mind when he was with her.

She smiled. "If you mean is it still growing, no. But it has an enormous capacity to nurture life."

Interesting observation. "Any idea how long ago it fell?"

"No. But from the tree's perspective, it was a recent event."

He cocked his head, studying her. It almost sounded like she was *talking* for the tree. Like it had given her the information and she had simply put it into a form he could understand. But that was crazy, wasn't it?

She pulled him closer, placing his palm on the bark, then covering his hand with hers. Her energy field engaged again, this time passing over his hand before connecting with the tree.

The sensation was quite different from the other times he'd felt her field. The warmth was still there, but the sensual overtones were not. This felt like... like...

He tried to put it into words, to give it a definition he could hold onto. But every word he chose came up woefully short. The closest description he could summon was how it would feel to be inside joy.

He also had a sensation of time beyond measure, of a depth of experience his brain struggled to comprehend. Was that coming from Libra? Or the tree? All he knew for certain was that he felt part of something vast, yet without feeling insignificant. It was electrifying. And humbling.

The sensation ebbed as Libra's energy field faded. She lifted his hand from the trunk and clasped it in hers. The look he'd seen earlier had returned to her eyes. "The tree likes you."

Her husky tone spoke to him on a deep level, too.

"Uh-huh." He didn't know how else to respond. His mind was still struggling to process what he'd experienced, and her switch in mood threw him off balance.

But his body caught up quickly when she led him into the tunnel beneath the tree and pulled him close for a kiss.

She laid claim to his mouth with a self-assurance that heated his blood, her energy field flowing over him as her tongue stroked across his lips once, twice, teasing, taunting. He responded in kind, drawing her flush against his body as his tongue met hers. Her answering shiver made him take the kiss deeper, tasting and tempting her lush mouth.

She moaned, pushing against his shoulders with surprising force, backing him up against the carved-out section of the tree. Once she had him pinned, her hands started roaming across his chest before tunneling under his shirt. The touch of her fingers and energy field against his bare skin made him tremble. When she brushed her fingernails over his nipples, another part of his anatomy strained against the fly of his jeans.

He broke contact with her mouth long enough to gasp for air. "You're driving me insane."

Her sultry chuckle almost brought him to his knees. "Is that a problem?"

The desire coursing through her called to him, his empathic senses lighting up like a solar flare. His mouth found hers again. Had he honestly thought of her as innocent? Because his petite vixen was showing him she could handle him just fine.

Sliding his hands down her body, he lifted her off the ground, settling her core against the bulge in his jeans.

Surprise flared in her emotional field.

He rocked forward. Her sharp inhale made him smile, as did the ripple of pleasure through her field. "Is that a problem for you?" he countered.

She answered him by wrapping her legs around his waist and pushing closer, a low moan rumbling in her throat.

Sanity threatened to take a vacation, but he clung to it with an iron grip. He was all for fun and games with her, but their first time making an intimate connection wasn't going to be up against a tree in the forest. He doubted that's what she had in mind, either. Her desire was rich and earthy, but unfocused. She wanted him, but without a specific endpoint.

Well, he had a very definite goal. Now that she was pressed against him, he wanted to hear her breathless cries as he took her over the edge.

Keeping a firm grip on her hips, he pivoted so that her back was now pressed to the tree. Her energy field flared, stealing the air he was working to force into his lungs.

Much more of that, and she'd make him come whether he planned to or not.

Lifting his head so he could watch her, he rocked forward again. Her eyes widened, her breath hitching.

"This is what you do to me, Libra," he murmured. It didn't take much effort to generate the sensations he was seeking. As an empath, he could easily tell exactly what pleased his partner. And Libra was the most responsive woman he'd ever held in his arms.

He kept up an easy rhythm, watching the excitement growing in her eyes, drinking in her moans and gasps as he exerted the right pressure at the best angle to draw maximum pleasure from her body. She trembled, her energy field expanding, adding a dimension to the erotic overtones he'd never experienced. But she didn't look away. She held his gaze like she could see into the center of his soul.

He felt the exact moment the first tremor hit. Her fingers dug into his shoulders as she arched against him. His body threatened to follow her as the wave gained force, but he held on, focusing all his attention on the pleasure rolling through her, making her shake in his arms.

Her eyes closed for a moment as her cry of release surrounded him. Then she slumped against his chest, her head on his shoulder.

He fought to fill his lungs with oxygen and to keep his erection from going off like a rocket. That was not how he wanted this interlude to end. It was too precious.

Holding her like this, making her come apart in his arms, felt like coming home.

Twenty-Two

Libra was no stranger to the concept of sex. The Suulh didn't have the kinds of social taboos or shaming associated with it that seemed fairly pervasive in Human culture. For Humans, concerns about accidental pregnancy and the passing of disease seemed to be the driving force behind many of the negative associations.

The Suulh didn't have to worry about either. As a race of natural healers, disease wasn't an issue, and pregnancy took a focused act of will. A Suulh child could only be conceived when both partners made a conscious decision prior to engaging in sex, and then only during the years of fertility, which started later and ended sooner than they did for Humans.

But all of that was academic knowledge. What she'd experienced with Brendan had surpassed all her expectations. The sensations of tension and pleasure had been intoxicating, her universe contracting to the point where his erection had stroked against her core, wringing responses from her body she couldn't stop if she'd wanted to.

And now that the wave had crested, she didn't want to move. If his strong arms weren't holding her up, she would have slid to the ground in a heap.

His erection still pressed against her, but he'd stopped moving, too. That puzzled her. According to what Marina and Gryphon had told her, both partners experienced release during sex. He clearly had not.

A thread of anxiety crept into her languid body. What if it was her fault? What if being Suulh meant she couldn't bring him to release? He'd proven he could meet her needs, but what if she couldn't do the same for him? Then they'd never be able to fully mate, or bear children.

"Hey." His soft voice wrapped around her as he rested his cheek on her hair. "Why the anxiety?"

She squeezed her eyes closed, her emotions fighting to gain traction. Would this be their only time together? Would he leave her, or would her failure force her to send him away because they couldn't be true mates, couldn't produce the next Sahzade?

"Libra?" He leaned back, clearly trying to get her to look at him.

She didn't want to. Didn't want to see the disappointment in his eyes. But it wasn't like he'd be able to hold her like this forever.

Lifting her head, she met his gaze.

But she didn't see disappointment, only confusion.

"Are you embarrassed?"

She frowned. "Why would I be embarrassed?"

"Uh, well, some women could be, after such an unusual first encounter."

Unusual first encounter. She was right. She'd failed him.

She tried to pull away, but the tree was still against her back and he hadn't loosened his grip on her hips. His erection, however, was fading fast.

"Libra, talk to me. What's going on?"

Fine. She'd face this like a Sahzade should, with courage and honesty, no matter how painful it might be.

She lifted her chin. "You didn't release."

He stared at her. "I didn't..." His brows drew down, his gaze searching hers like the answers to his questions were written behind her eyes. Then his lips slowly curled. "Is that what this is about? You're worried because I didn't come?"

"You should have released. I may be an incompatible mate for you."

"Incompatible?" His smile grew and his shoulders shook. "Libra, my love, I've never been more compatible with anyone in my life."

Now it was her turn to frown. "Then why didn't you release?"

He shook his head, his eyes sparkling. "It didn't seem like the gentlemanly thing to do, considering. It also would have been awkward to walk into the cabin with a damp spot on the front of my jeans."

She still wasn't clear what he was saying. "So, you could have released, but you chose not to?" She'd never heard of that happening before, either.

He ducked his head, his shoulders still shaking, but when he met her gaze, the heat burning in the depths of his eyes sparked a matching flame in her core. "It was a Herculean task, I assure you. And next time we do this, I definitely plan to release."

A bubble of hope lifted her up. "Next time?"

"Oh, yes." He drifted closer, his mouth millimeters from hers. "There will certainly be a next time." His lips stroked hers. "Many more next times."

Her anxiety gave way under the power of his kiss. She hadn't failed him. He'd been acting protective of her in some way. She still didn't understand, but his promise that he could reach fulfillment when he chose to was good enough for now. Especially when she considered the many more next times awaiting them.

Lifting his head, he gave her a long look before gingerly setting her back on her feet. "You are a very tempting woman, Libra Hawke." He captured her hand and laced their fingers together. "And while I love this setting, next time I want a bed nearby. Are there any hotels or B&Bs in the town we're going to tonight?"

Tonight. A tremor of excitement raced through her. Next time could be as soon as tonight! "There's a small hotel on the main street. And one of our customers owns a B&B."

"Oh? Have you ever been there?"

"No. But Gryphon and Marina have. During the summer months they drop off food mid-week to a few local businesses."

"If they have a room available, would you be interested in going there with me tonight after our date?"

Her pulse leapt, her imagination painting a vivid picture of the possibilities.

But she also had work to do. "I have to be at the market by eight tomorrow morning."

"That's fine. I'd make sure we got there on time." His voice deepened as he pulled her closer. "Tell me, Libra. Do you want to spend the night with me?"

Her body tingled from head to toe, her energy field hovering below the surface of her skin. An entire night with Brendan, alone in a room with no distractions.

She wanted it more than she'd wanted anything in her life.

"Yes."

Twenty-Three

Gryphon and Marina shocked Brendan by not raising an eyebrow when Libra announced their change of plans for the evening. Marina almost looked smug, like she'd anticipated this outcome from the beginning.

While Libra headed to her room to get ready for their date, Brendan contacted the B&B through the comm panel. The woman he spoke with confirmed she had several openings, but she recommended the garret room because it was the most private. He also discovered their dinner location was walking distance from the B&B, an added bonus.

He slipped into the bathroom to change and gather his overnight bag. When he returned to the living room, he found Libra waiting for him.

The sight froze him in his tracks. Up to now, she'd always been dressed in jeans or lounge pants and a sweater or sweatshirt. But she'd traded them in for a long-sleeved turquoise-blue dress that skimmed over her curves and flowed gracefully to mid-calf.

Her golden hair tumbled over her shoulders in a river of curls, the silken strands begging to be touched.

"Brendan?" She frowned, taking a step closer. "Are you okay?"

He must have been staring a lot longer than he'd realized. He gave himself a mental shake. "I'm great." He met her halfway, lifting her hand to his lips. "You look beautiful," he murmured.

A shiver of excitement danced through her emotional field as his lips brushed across the soft skin on the back of her hand. "Thank you."

"No, thank you." His gaze swept over her again. "Tonight, I'm the luckiest man on Earth."

Her cheeks tinged pink, but she smiled.

The rumble of Gryphon clearing his throat made him turn toward the kitchen.

Gryphon and Marina stood by the stove while Lelindia perched on one of the barstools, their focus on him and Libra.

"So, we'll meet you two at the market at eight." Gryphon looked like he was trying to be serious while holding back a grin. His emotions made it clear he wanted the evening to go well for them. "But if you run late—"

"We won't be late." Brendan didn't want that to be the precedent they'd set, letting Gryphon and Marina shoulder extra work while he and Libra played. If everything went the way he hoped, he'd have many more opportunities to spend the night with Libra. He didn't have to squeeze it all in tonight.

Gryphon smiled. "Okay." His gaze shifted to Libra. "Have fun."

Her eyes twinkled and her voice deepened. "I intend to."

Okay, then.

Brendan helped her with her coat, pulled on his, then picked up their overnight bags and followed her out the door. The cool air invigorated him as they strolled down the path to where their transport waited. He dropped the bags in the trunk before joining Libra in the back seat.

She scooted over next to him, resting her head on his shoulder as the transport started down the driveway to the road. Her soft sigh of contentment filled him with happiness.

"Is that a new dress?" he asked.

"Mm-hm. Marina and Lelindia helped me pick it out after we finished at the market."

"It looks wonderful on you."

She snuggled closer, her arm slipping inside his coat to wrap around his waist. "You look wonderful, too."

The tactile sensation of her body pressed against his in the shadowed confines of the transport made it difficult to focus on making conversation, or the dinner and dancing he'd promised her, especially when he knew a comfortable bed awaited them at their destination. Maybe he'd leave their bags at the front desk when they checked in. He didn't trust himself to walk into their room and make it back out, not with Libra beside him.

She seemed to be doing a much better job of managing her reactions than he was. In fact, her emotional state reminded him of an athlete's focused excitement before a big competition, rather than the nervousness and uncertainty he usually sensed during a first date.

Then again, they were already living under the same roof and sharing meals, so this wasn't like any first date he'd ever been on before. And he'd certainly never suggested to any of the women he'd dated that they spend the night together this early in the relationship. But with Libra it had seemed like the perfect time. He had no doubts, and thankfully, neither did she.

He slid his arm around her shoulders, drawing her in. "It's hard to believe we've only known each other for two days."

Her arm tightened around his waist. "I know."

But holding her like this, it was impossible to imagine his life without her in it. Sometime soon, they'd need to have a serious discussion about what their future together might look like. She still had no idea what his work entailed, or how the resources he commanded could open all kinds of doors for her. And Gryphon and Marina, too, if they were interested. For Libra, it would mean leaving the simple life she had here, but he felt certain once she understood how much he could give her in exchange, she'd take the leap.

And it wasn't like she couldn't still spend time here. He'd happily buy the property the cabin was on so they could still use it.

He needed to formulate a plan for how he'd broach the subject. But not tonight. He wanted this night to be all about her.

The B&B turned out to be a charming three-story structure a couple blocks from the main road through town. The tang of salt in the air signaled they were fairly close to the coastline.

Libra insisted on carrying her own overnight bag so she could hold his hand as they walked up the steps to the front door. The wreath hanging in the center of the door looked similar to the one she'd crafted the night before, and the one hanging on the front door of the cabin. "Did you make this?"

She nodded. "A couple weeks ago."

Good to know the local residents appreciated her talents. He opened the door and ushered her inside.

A small reception desk sat to their left next to a carved wood staircase. He set down his bag beside Libra's and moved to the open doorway behind the desk. "Hello?"

"Coming!" Footsteps preceded the arrival of a tall woman with greying blonde shoulder-length hair and a trim figure. Her face lit up when she saw Libra. "What a gorgeous dress."

Clearly the woman had never seen Libra in a dress before, either.

Libra handled the compliment with an easy smile. "Thank you."

The woman turned to him. "I'm Joan. You must be Brendan."

"Guilty as charged. Thank you for accommodating us on such short notice."

"Of course. Happy to have you." She moved behind the reception desk. "Do you want one set of keys or two?"

He looked to Libra for guidance.

"One set is fine," she replied.

"Alrighty." Joan held up a keyring with two keys and a circular disc with the B&B's name carved into it. "This one will open your room, and this one unlocks the front door. I lock up at nine, so if you come back later than that, you'll need to let yourselves in."

Brendan accepted the keys. "I also have a favor to ask. Would you mind keeping our bags here at the desk until we get back?" He paused, his brain alerting him that he didn't have a logical reason to give for the request. He certainly didn't want to tell her the truth, that he didn't trust himself in a room with Libra and a bed. "We're both pretty hungry, and eager to get to the restaurant."

Joan's smile, and the emotions that accompanied it, told him he hadn't fooled her one bit. She'd probably fielded stranger requests, and knew exactly what most of her guests were focused on when they checked in. She was the one who'd recommended the privacy of the garret room, after all. "I'll do you one better. You go ahead and I'll take your bags up to the room myself."

"Oh, I don't—"

"It's no trouble. Your door is at the top of the stairs." She ushered them toward the entrance. "Enjoy your dinner."

He hesitated for a moment, until Joan winked at him as she reached for his bag. "Thank you."

"You're welcome."

As soon as they were outside, Libra clasped his hand in hers, a small sigh escaping her lips. "This is perfect."

He gazed down at her, the soft glow from the streetlamps making her golden curls shine like a halo. His angel. His beautiful, passionate angel. "My thoughts exactly."

"In case I forget to say it later, thank you for a wonderful evening."

He grinned. "You're that sure it will be wonderful?"

She smiled, but the look in her eyes was serious. "Yes, I am."

What a gift. "Thank you for saying that."

She squeezed his hand, a wave of giddy happiness flowing off her.

As they strolled along the sidewalk, she pointed out several businesses whose proprietors would be visiting their booth at the market the next day.

"Do you ever have trouble keeping up with the demand?"

"Sometimes. In the summer, especially. The greenhouse ends up looking like a jungle. We've come up with as many creative ways as we can to add more plants vertically, since we can't expand the footprint of the space. But we make sure we always have something for our repeat customers."

She clearly enjoyed her work, and the good will it generated with members of the community. He'd need to factor that in when he broached the idea of a future together. With a little planning, he could probably arrange blocks of a couple months once or twice a year that they could spend here.

A rustic log structure appeared around the curve of the street, lights across the peaked roof and along the inclined railing of the walkway illuminating the front entrance. An equally rustic sign out front confirmed they'd reached Redwoods.

A country beat drifted out as Brendan held the door open for Libra. Rich aromas and cozy warmth greeted them as they stepped inside.

A young man who looked just out of high school smiled as they walked up to the hosting station. "Table for two?"

"Please. Something near the dance floor, if possible."

"Of course. This way."

Bypassing the main room behind him, he led them into the bar area. A row of booths sat opposite two sides of the U-shaped bar. The third side held a small raised platform for the live band and a space for dancing. Several couples were already twirling around to the lively country music.

"How's this?" the young man asked, gesturing to a booth near a fireplace built into the wall that joined the bar to the main dining room, providing ambience to both.

Libra looked as lit up as the fireplace. "It's perfect."

Brendan grinned. "Yep. Perfect."

The young man beamed at them, setting their menus down after they'd slid into the booth. "Have you dined with us before?"

Brendan glanced at Libra, who shook her head. "Nope," he replied. "This is our first time."

"Then let me recommend you save room for dessert. Our baker makes a chocolate cake that's to die for."

"Thanks. We'll keep that in mind."

"Your server will be with you shortly."

After the young man left, Brendan rested his forearms on the table and gazed at Libra. "Have I mentioned how beautiful you look tonight?"

Her slow smile made him want to kiss her lush lips. "Yes, you have."

"Good. It bears repeating."

He glanced over the menu, not really caring what he ordered. He was here for the company and the opportunity to dance with Libra, not the food. When Libra gave her order to their server, he doubled it.

After the young woman left, he held his hand out. "Ready for your next dancing lesson?"

Libra glanced at the dance floor, her expression wary. "This music is a lot faster than what you played last night."

"I know." He dropped his voice to a throaty rumble. "But I promise you'll have fun."

That did the trick. Heat flared in her eyes. "I have no doubt."

Zing! His angel could give as well as she took. He stood, trying to keep his tone casual. "Then follow me."

She placed her hand in his, her warmth drawing him closer without conscious thought. He guided her to the edge of the dance floor, which was relatively clear of other dancers. He showed her the basic steps, which she picked up as quickly as she'd learned the waltz the previous night. And then she was in his arms again.

The rest of the room blurred, the chatter of voices, even the steady beat of the music just a subtle background to the sensations Libra's touch generated. Her palm caressed his as they moved in perfect harmony, first with the basic steps, and then with greater and greater flair as her laughter urged him to get creative, spinning and twirling her around the floor. By the time the song ended, they were both breathless.

The sparkle in her eyes matched the joy flowing off her in waves. "Can we stay for another?"

As if she had to ask. "Of course."

The tempo changed, the band switching to a waltz. Libra's smile grew. "I know this one." She moved into position, her left hand settling on his arm, her right nestling into his left. Sliding his right hand around her narrow waist, he pulled her closer before leading her into the dance.

Talk about perfection. As the music swirled around them, he felt like he'd been dancing with her his whole life. The growing awareness in her turquoise eyes didn't hurt, either. It was making him think about a very different type of dancing. One that wasn't suitable for a public venue.

By the time the waltz ended, he needed a break before he embarrassed himself. He nodded toward the table. "Can we head back? Our food should be out soon."

Her half-smile let him know she'd felt the evidence of his physical reaction and had figured out why he wanted to sit. "Of course."

And that was another thing. She had the most forthright attitude regarding sex he'd ever encountered. Their frank discussion this afternoon had floored him, and her easy use of sexual innuendo kept turning the tables on him. Not at all what he'd expected, considering yesterday she'd hidden behind a tree to spy on him.

Had it only been yesterday? Gazing at her now, that didn't seem possible.

Libra sipped from her water glass, watching him over the rim. The look in her eyes wasn't helping with his condition. "When did you learn to dance?"

Good. A nice, safe topic. "When I was a kid. Both my parents loved to dance. And sing. That's how they met, actually. My mom was performing at a benefit concert where my dad's company was one of the sponsors. When he saw her on stage he was captivated. He asked her out that night. They were wed within a month."

"They most have bonded quickly."

Bonded. Interesting choice of words. "I suppose they did. Mom always said she'd known Dad was the one for her by the way he'd approached her after her performance. Most men either tried to flatter her because of her talent, or acted like they were in awe of her. Dad had acted like she was his long-lost best friend. She'd been as smitten as he was."

Libra sighed. "They were very blessed."

He nodded. "They lived a life of joy together, and died together, doing something that mattered to them." He gazed at her, a soft melancholy swelling inside. "I'm just sorry they never had the opportunity to meet you. They would have loved you."

The words tumbled out of his mouth before he considered the possible implications. Mentioning meeting the parents often created tension this early in a relationship. He paused, waiting to see how she'd react.

Once again, she surprised him. A melancholy similar to his own brushed up against him. "My parents would have loved you, too."

The yearning in her voice made his heart ache. Losing his parents had been hard, and unexpected, but she'd been a child when hers had died. Old enough to understand what she'd lost but too young to effectively process her pain on her own.

He reached his arm across the table, palm up. She placed her hand in his, the tactile connection going straight to his soul. Bonded. That's the term she'd used to describe his parents. And exactly how he felt about her.

"I've got two black bean burgers with wedge-cut fries, and two chamomile hot teas."

The server's cheerful voice broke the mood. Brendan released Libra's hand and sat back. "That's us."

They switched to less intense topics while they ate, like why plants enchanted her so much, and why he loved to fly. Their answers were remarkably similar, focusing on the euphoria they experienced, and the energizing effect of learning new things. He also found out she liked mustard with her fries, and had only tasted beer once.

"Once?"

She nodded, dipping a fry in the pool of mustard and popping it into her mouth. "The customer who gave it to us raved about it, but it tasted awful, bitter. Another customer gave us a bottle of tequila once, too, as a holiday present. That tasted better, but it didn't affect me the way it does Hu–" She coughed. "Huge sections of the population. I didn't feel any different, which seems to be the point."

He gazed at her. "Are you saying alcohol doesn't make you intoxicated?" He'd never heard of such a thing.

She shrugged, glancing away. "Doesn't seem to."

Well, wasn't that intriguing? Could her energy work somehow neutralize the effects? He couldn't see how, but he also didn't understand the extent of her abilities, either. "Have you tried wine?" That would be an important piece of information to know. He had a pretty extensive wine cellar at home, which he kept well-stocked.

"Oh, yes. That I like. Sometimes Gryphon will serve local wines instead of tea with dinner."

Good to know. He could have a few cases delivered as a thank you for letting him stay.

The server stopped by the table to check on them. "Did you save room for dessert?"

He glanced at Libra, lifting a brow.

She had a mischievous twinkle in her eye. "The chocolate cake sounded nice."

He thought so, too, but he was the one with the chocolate addiction, not her. "Do you want your own slice, or should we share?"

"Let's share."

He turned to the server. "One slice of chocolate cake and two forks, please."

"You've got it."

As the server walked away, he nudged Libra's foot with his. "You're up to something. What's going on behind those lovely eyes?"

She smiled. "I figured I should sample their cake so I can report back to Gryphon. He'll want to know how their desserts compare to his."

"Ah. So, your choice had nothing to do with my love affair with chocolate?"

"Well, maybe a little."

"Thanks for that."

"You're welcome." She looked over her shoulder at the dance floor. It was more crowded now, and all the seats at the bar were filled. "Can we dance a little more first?"

"Absolutely." He captured her hand as she slid out of the booth, leading her to the floor. The band started up a new number, which was a line dance he recognized. He positioned her next to him. "Stay beside me and do what I do."

"Okay."

He joined in with the rest of the group, talking her through the steps as they followed the beat. Libra's face tightened in concentration the first time through, but by the second repetition she was with him, and by the third, her movements became fluid, the sway of her hips and slight shimmy of her shoulders distracting him. He almost bumped into the man beside him, who resembled a scale model of Paul Bunyan.

"Sorry."

The other man grunted, glancing over his shoulder at him, and then at Libra.

The flow of Libra's emotions wasn't helping him focus, either. She was totally in the moment, happiness and sensual pleasure pouring off her, her lilting laugh making him want to pull her into his arms and kiss her senseless.

Instead, he gave her an intentional bump with his hip, which elicited another shower of laughter. As the dance turned them around, she copied his move, tapping his hip with hers and adding a little wiggle that almost popped his eyes out of his head.

Her throaty chuckle made it clear that was exactly the reaction she'd been going for.

As the music drew to a close, he circled his arm around her waist, reeling her in. "Keep that up, pretty lady, and I'll forget all about dessert."

She moved gracefully into his arms as the band changed to a slow tune. "Wouldn't want that. At least, not yet."

The promise in her eyes made his skin flush. "Soon. I wa—"

A hand landed on his shoulder, halting their movement. "Cuttin' in," a deep voice, slightly slurred, informed him.

He turned his head. Paul Bunyan was looming over him, his gaze on Libra. The look in the man's eyes was troubling, but not as much as the emotions coming off him. Suppressed rage, a deep sense of loss, and a solid dose of lust smacked each other like rams butting heads.

Brendan tightened his grip, pivoting Libra slightly to shield her. "Sorry, friend, the lady's with me."

Bunyan's fingers dug into his shoulder. "I said, I'm cuttin' in."

Fear rose off Libra in a cloud, her reaction in direct proportion to the anger in his own chest. "That's up to the lady, and she doesn't want to dance with you."

The pressure on his shoulder increased. He'd have bruises in the morning.

"Says you." Bunyan held out his free hand to Libra. "Let me show you how to dance with a real man."

The alcohol content of the man's breath could cause second-hand intoxication. Great. He was dealing with a drunk hothead built like a truck.

Libra pressed against him, her arms snaking around his waist from behind. Her fear vibrated like a livewire, kicking his protective instincts into high gear. But he wasn't a physical match for this jerk. He'd have to use his head. "I told you, friend, she's not interested. Why don't I buy you a cup of coffee?" Not that it would make a dent in the bender this guy had going.

Bunyan shoved against his shoulder, forcing him to back up a step. "I don't want coffee. I want to dance with her!" He jabbed a finger over Brendan's shoulder.

He stood his ground. "She's not interested."

The hand the man had jabbed in Libra's direction closed into a fist and took aim at his head.

The move was so telegraphed that he could have easily avoided it, but not with Bunyan holding him in place with one hand and Libra blocking him in from behind.

Another hand grabbed Bunyan's elbow, holding back the punch.

Thankfully, the man attached to that hand was almost as solidly built as Bunyan. He was dressed in a dark brown collared shirt with the restaurant logo embroidered on the front. "I'm the manager.

Is there a problem here, folks?" His voice was genial, but his emotions made it clear he'd correctly assessed the situation and wasn't about to let a brawl break out during the dinner hour.

Bunyan turned his ire on the manager, but his glower receded when he got a good look at his new opponent. Some of the bravado left his voice. "Just wanted to dance with the lady," he muttered.

The man gave him a closed-mouth smile. "I think you should consider calling it a night, instead." It wasn't a suggestion.

Bunyan's mouth worked, like he had some choice words he wanted to share. But common sense, or more likely the desire to stay out of jail, won out. "Whatever."

Releasing his grip on Brendan's shoulder with a parting shove, he pulled free from the manager's grasp, stomped over to the bar to grab his coat, and stormed through the crowd to the front door.

The manager watched him go with a sigh before turning to Brendan and Libra. "I'm very sorry, folks. Are you okay?"

Libra continued to cling to him, but her fear level was dropping, replaced by something that felt like guilt. He rested his hands over hers, noting the slight tremble in her arms. "We're okay. Thanks for stepping in."

"I hope this won't color your view of our restaurant. I'll be comping your meal, but is there anything else I can get you?"

He glanced over his shoulder at Libra. Her eyes were wide, her body trembling as she stared at the spot where the man had disappeared. "I think we'll sit for a little while."

The manager nodded. "I'll send your server over to fetch anything you might need. Again, I'm very sorry."

Brendan summoned a smile. "Not your fault. And I appreciate your help." Gingerly unwinding Libra's hands from his waist, he clasped her hand in his and led her to their table.

The cake slice and two forks sat in the middle of the table. He didn't feel like eating it now, but the chocolate might help soothe Libra's agitation.

Instead of settling on the opposite side of the table, he slid in next to her, making contact from toe to shoulder. She was still shaking, and hadn't said a word.

Their server appeared a second later, her face pale and her smile weak. "Is there anything I can get you?"

He glanced at the tea mugs, which were now close to empty. "How about more tea?" If memory served, chamomile was supposed to be soothing, too.

"Right away."

Brendan slid his arm around Libra's shoulder, pulling her close. "I'm sorry you had to go through that."

She finally lifted her gaze. She looked shell-shocked. "He was going to hit you."

"He was going to try."

"And I... I..." She looked around the room, like she was searching for something. Or trying to hide from someone. "I didn't know what to do."

"You didn't need to do anything."

"But he could have hurt you." Indignation and anger shot off her like sparks.

But it was the underlying guilt that dug at him. "Better me than you."

Twenty-Four

Libra stared at Brendan as shame and guilt darkened her vision. He didn't understand. Couldn't understand.

For the first time in her adult life, she'd faced a moment of decision as a Sahzade. And she'd failed. She'd cracked like an egg, unable to handle the potential consequences if she acted.

Instead, she'd cowered in fear, leaving Brendan exposed to danger.

He trailed his fingers along her cheek. "You were afraid."

Not afraid. Terrified. But not of the man threatening them. She'd been trapped in a room full of people who would witness what she could do if she stopped the attack. She'd been terrified of exposing her secret for all to see.

And now she was angry. Enraged at herself. She'd been prepared to let that horrid man hurt Brendan, rather than risk discovery. What kind of Sahzade was she?

Unworthy. Pathetic. Brendan wasn't a Suulh, but that didn't matter. A true Sahzade never allowed harm to come to those under her protection, no matter the cost. Her mother and grandmother had taught her that from the day she was born. If they had lived to see her now, they would be so disappointed.

"Hey." Brendan's thumb caressed her cheek, tracing the line of moisture from her eyes. "It's okay, Libra. We're okay."

She shook her head, not trusting herself to speak. He deserved so much better. So much more.

"Here's your tea." The server's voice was soft, cautious, as she set the two mugs on the table.

"Thank you," Libra mumbled, keeping her gaze on the mug in front of her.

"Can I get you folks anything else?"

"No, we're good. Thank you." Brendan's voice was soothing, filled with calm assurance.

Which made her feel more miserable.

Wrapping her hands around her mug, she allowed the heat to burn into her palms. It matched the anger and guilt burning in her chest.

Brendan's arm tightened on her shoulder. "Libra, what's wrong? I know you're upset that that man tried to hit me, but—"

"It's not that."

"It's not?"

She still couldn't look at him. "I should have protected you."

He was silent for so long she finally glanced up.

Confusion clouded his blue eyes and his brow furrowed with concern. "How could you have protected me?"

She opened her mouth, then closed it. What could she say? Nothing that he would understand. She'd only make the situation worse.

He sighed, his lips turning down. "It's perfectly natural to feel fear when confronted by an aggressive person who poses a physical threat. Please don't blame yourself for reacting the way you did."

Rather than letting her off the hook, his words poked new needles under her skin. If he knew the truth, he wouldn't be making excuses for her. "You don't understand."

"I'm trying to."

Yes, he was. And her behavior was making him work even harder. "I know. I'm sorry."

His frown faded away. "You have nothing to be sorry for."

Oh, yes, she did. But ruining what was left of their evening wasn't fair to him. For now, she needed to suppress the emotions that were causing him anxiety. She could continue her self-flagellation later.

Picking up one of the forks, she poised it over the slice of cake. "We still need to complete our research project so we can report to Gryphon."

A ghost of his smile returned. "So we do." He picked up the other fork, tapped it lightly against hers, then took a bite of the cake.

She followed suit. It wasn't bad. Not nearly as good as Gryphon's creations, but she could see why it was popular.

She met his gaze. "What do you think?"

He chewed slowly as he made his evaluation. "It's good." He gave her a wink. "But Gryphon could do better."

That coaxed a tiny smile to her lips. "My thoughts exactly."

By the time they'd finished the dessert and their tea, she had her emotions under control, locked away in the impenetrable vault she'd created as a child.

Before they left, Brendan pulled a credit square from his pocket, posting a hefty tip to their server and thanking her as they passed her on their way out the door.

The temperature had dropped, but was still comfortable enough for strolling down the street, especially after Brendan slid his arm around her shoulders.

"Right now, there's nowhere I'd rather be than here with you," he murmured.

The moon had risen, the light painting streamers of silver in his blond hair and adding a sparkle to his eyes. The sight kindled the heat in her blood, reminding her that they were heading back to a private room. "And there's nowhere—"

"I said I want to dance with her."

The harsh voice locked Libra's feet to the sidewalk.

Brendan froze beside her, his grip tightened on her shoulders as they both turned.

A large shadow emerged from the dark alley between two buildings.

This time, fear wasn't the emotion that boiled up inside her as the oversized brute swaggered toward them, a glass bottle held loosely in his fingers.

"No one to save you now, pretty boy," he snarled, glaring at Brendan like he was the source of all his problems. "The lady's goin' home with me."

She stepped forward at the same time Brendan tugged on her shoulder to push her behind him, resulting in a stalemate.

"She's not going anywhere with you. You need to go home and sleep it off."

Brendan increased the pressure on her shoulder, pushing her back, but she fought against him, trying to get past him.

The man sneered. "Looks like she doesn't agree with you."

Brendan shot her a quick glance. She could see the fear and confusion in his eyes, could almost hear his unspoken plea. *Let me protect you.*

But he wasn't the one who could keep them safe.

She faced the behemoth advancing on them, her words as cool as the winter breeze. "Leave us alone."

The man blinked, startled by her tone. Then the idiot actually tried to give her what he must have thought was a charming smile. "Oh, come on, little lady. I'm twice the man he is." The smile turned into a leer. "I'll prove it to you."

His implication made her skin crawl, adding fire to the furnace in her belly. "You're not *half* the man he is. I'm not going anywhere with you."

The leer disappeared, turning into a glower. "You think you're too good for me? You're just like her. But I'll show you."

Changing his grip on the bottle, he lifted his arm and swung, aiming for Brendan's head.

White-hot rage blasted through her, erupting like a volcano. She was out of Brendan's grasp in a millisecond, her energy field flaring to life and her shield solidifying on the leading edge as she darted between him and their attacker.

The bottle struck the shield and shattered. The man's arm and shoulder hit the shield next, and he howled in pain. Staggering back, he stared at Brendan in shock, then with pure hatred. "You—"

Whatever he was going to say was lost in a guttural roar as he charged, the jagged edge of the bottle moving toward Brendan's throat.

Her rage hit a fever pitch. Swiping her arm, she smashed her shield into the man's outstretched hand with enough force to break bone, the bottle slicing across his palm before clattering to the sidewalk.

He screamed, swaying on his feet as blood welled on his injured hand.

She advanced on him, her energy field crackling around her, her shield pulsing in time with the fury pounding in every cell of her body. "I told you to leave us alone!" She struck again, smacking her shield against his side, toppling him to the ground like a felled tree.

His eyes looked like twin moons as he lay on his side, staring up at her, his bleeding hand held protectively in front of his face.

Which cooled the heat of her rage, bringing it to a low simmer. He didn't look tough now. Or menacing. He looked like a frightened little boy who'd spotted a monster looming over his bed.

Fine. If that's what it took to get his attention, she'd be the monster. "You're drunk, but that's no excuse. Attacking people is wrong." He'd also mentioned a her, which gave a clue as to what might have triggered his aggressive behavior. "And when a woman tells you no, she means NO. Got it?" She smacked his shoulder with her shield to emphasize the point.

He nodded rapidly, his eyes getting bigger by the second.

No wonder. As a Human, he couldn't see her shield. As far as he was concerned, the effect she was having on him was magic, or maybe the work of a poltergeist or vengeful spirit, not something corporeal.

She drew in a slow breath, calming her mind. No one would blame her if she left him bleeding on the sidewalk, but Marina would be disappointed. A Sahzade protected the weak, even from themselves. And this man was definitely weak.

Kneeling, she held out her hand. "Give me your hand."

He recoiled, but his terror kept him from getting up and running away.

She sighed. "I'm not going to hurt you. I'm going to heal your injuries."

His gaze flicked briefly to his hand, then back to her.

He seemed incapable of deciding which option was less likely to end in more pain, so she chose for him. Reaching out, she clasped his hand in both of hers, summoning the healing field that allowed her to begin restoring the damaged cells to health.

She felt the jolt of his body as she drove her energy into his skin and bone, but his fear worked in her favor. He held perfectly still as she focused on repairing his hand. The result wouldn't be nearly as complete as what Marina could do, but good enough that he wouldn't suffer any permanent damage. Thank goodness the bone breaks were clean and the cuts weren't deep. And that they were on his hand, where energy centers were naturally enhanced, even in Humans.

As soon as the underlying trauma was repaired, she released her hold and stood.

He stared at his hand, turning it back and forth, examining the red spots that had been cuts minutes before and flexing his fingers to test the bones.

"Now, go home and get some sleep."

His gaze moved to her, his paralysis breaking in a rush. With surprising speed, he lumbered to his feet and took off down the sidewalk, looking over his shoulder right before he turned the corner out of sight.

Leaving her alone with Brendan, who hadn't said a word since the attack began.

Steeling herself, she pivoted to face him.

Twenty-Five

Brendan stared at Libra, his mind whirling like a tornado. "What was that?"

He'd known she was a talented energy worker, but what he'd just witnessed defied categorization. Her energy field had changed, solidified when the bottle had struck, and again when she'd gone on the offensive.

But that wasn't as disturbing as the primal rage he'd felt blasting off her, or the fact that she'd fought with the easy grace of muscle memory. Someone had trained her, taught her how to use her energy abilities as a weapon.

Yet she'd healed the damage she'd caused, acting like it was the most natural thing in the world.

She stayed where she was, her hands at her sides and her chin lifted. "He was going to hurt you."

"I know." And she'd defended him like a momma bear guarding her cub. He needed to remember that. Her desire to protect him had triggered her reaction. "But what *was* that?"

She sighed, her gaze drifting up to the stars, a sense of deep loss and resignation replacing her anger. "It's not something I talk about."

Her pain pulled him two steps closer. "Why not?"

"It's in the past."

She might want to believe that, but her reaction told him her subconscious was keeping it very much in the present.

Her expression flattened out, her eyes growing dull. "We can go back to the cabin."

"The cabin?" Not at all where his thoughts were heading. "I don't want to go to the cabin. I want you to talk to me."

She shook her head, stuffing her hands in her pockets. "I can't."

She was closing herself off, shutting him out. He couldn't let her do that, either.

He crossed the distance between them, catching her off guard as he pulled her into his arms.

She stiffened, pushing away.

"Please, don't," he whispered, tightening his grip. "It's okay. It'll be okay."

She stilled, her emotions bobbing like a boat on a stormy sea. "It will?"

"Yes." Holding her, creating a tactile affirmation of their connection, seemed the most effective way to make his point. "Just don't shut me out."

She was silent for a long moment. When she tilted her head up to meet his gaze, wariness lurked in her eyes. "You're not afraid of me?"

"Why would I be afraid of you?"

"Because…" Anxiety and sadness dominated her emotional field. "Because I'm different."

"Yes, you are." He'd used that word to describe her earlier. At the time, he hadn't understood how right he was. She was unlike anyone he'd ever met. And her abilities were rocking the foundation of his reality. "But that doesn't scare me."

"It doesn't?"

He shook his head. Her abilities had shocked him, but her quick action may have saved his life. And despite the power of her rage, as soon as she'd disarmed their attacker, she'd pulled back. Calmed down. Offered assistance. That showed self-restraint, and compassion. "But I would like to know more about your abilities."

She pursed her lips, her gaze sweeping up and down the empty street. "Not here."

"Fair enough." Releasing his grip, he slid his hand into hers and turned in the direction of the B&B. "We'll wait until we're in our room."

She shot him sidelong glances as they walked along the sidewalk, her anxiety hovering like a cloud.

He focused on staying calm, not wanting to add to her stress level. Hopefully talking things through would provide clarity and give him some clues on how to help her process what they'd gone through. And give him answers as to what exactly she could do.

Pulling out the keys, he unlocked the front door of the B&B and led the way up the stairs. Turning left at the landing, he opened their door, revealing another flight of stairs, narrower and enclosed, climbing up into the garret room.

Soft light greeted them from two wall sconces, giving the room a welcoming glow. A spacious bed with a plush comforter and fluffy white pillows enclosed by an antique wood headboard and footboard claimed most of the space. A small couch and upholstered chair sat opposite the bed, and a bistro table with two chairs was tucked into a corner near the door to the private bath.

An hour ago, all he would have been focused on was getting Libra stretched out naked on that bed. But that was before he'd watched her take down a man twice her size using her energy field.

Libra stopped beside him, the tenor of her emotions still firmly locked on anxiety as her gaze swept the room. "It's lovely."

And she was as nervous as a cat in a room full of rocking chairs.

He set the keys on the dresser near the door, removed his coat and shoes, and turned to face her. "Why don't we sit on the couch."

She nodded slowly, but after she took off her coat and shoes, her shoulders started hiking their way up toward her ears.

He clasped her hand, drawing her to the couch and settling into one corner. She perched beside him, her body so far forward she was in danger of sliding onto the floor.

Slipping his arm around her waist, he tugged softly. "Come here," he coaxed, drawing her back into the crook of his arm.

She didn't resist, but her body had all the fluidity of a mannequin as her back pressed against his chest. Apparently she didn't want to look at him. That was fine, for now. Talking about this would probably be easier for her without direct eye contact.

He laced the fingers of his right hand through hers, stroking her skin with his thumb. Keeping his voice calm and neutral, he posed his first question, the one he already had a pretty good idea how she'd answer. "So, you can manipulate your energy field to form a solid barrier?"

Her mannequin-like fingers stiffened. "Yes."

He kept up the gentle touch, relaxing his own body as fully as he could, hoping she'd take her cues from him. "And you can project it some distance from your body?" Again, he'd seen her do it, but having her confirm it gave him an intro to the tougher questions.

"Yes."

"Is there a limit to how far you can push it?" Because his mind had started filling in blanks during the walk. The moment right after his plane had touched down on the road, when he'd seen a flash of white and felt a hard jolt of collision, was taking on a whole new perspective.

She hesitated. "Yes, there's a limit."

"I'm guessing you can manage at least a few meters though, correct?"

Guilt joined the anxiety flowing off her. Her answer was barely audible. "Yes." She turned her head, not enough to meet his gaze, but far enough he could see the tension on her face. "I didn't mean to hurt you. I didn't know you were there until..." Her chin dipped, the guilt gaining ground.

"Until it was too late?" he finished for her.

She nodded, pain weaving into the guilt and anxiety. "I reacted on instinct."

So, he was right. She'd been in the middle of the road, and had raised her shield, deflecting his plane into the tree. The raw power in that answer floored him. And the depth of her pain and guilt hollowed out his gut.

He slid his other arm around her waist, pulling her closer. "Please don't blame yourself. If you hadn't used your shield, my plane would have killed you." His mind tossed up an image of that reality, fear jabbing his solar plexus like a blunt knife.

She made a snuffle that was part snort, part sigh. "No, it wouldn't have."

What? Her absolute certainty unnerved him, flipping his mental image on its head. "Are you saying if the plane had struck you, you could have survived? Healed yourself?" That couldn't be true, could it?

Her anxiety took center stage again, like she'd revealed more than she'd intended.

Which generated anxiety for him, too. Part of him wanted to stop asking questions, stop learning the answers. She'd already cracked the seals on his reality. But burying his head in the sand wouldn't get him where he wanted to go. A relationship without trust and honesty wasn't a relationship at all.

"Libra, please trust me." He'd thought they'd gotten over the biggest hurdles, but larger ones kept appearing. "I promise I'll keep your secrets safe. No matter what."

Her breathing grew harsher, the emotional struggle he could feel her waging producing physical reactions.

He wanted to help her work through the roadblocks, which meant keeping her talking. "Can I ask more specific questions about the extent of your ability to self-heal?"

She didn't say no.

He plunged ahead. "Can you heal any type of skin damage?"

"Yes."

"Broken bones?" A collision with a plane would definitely result in broken bones.

"Yes."

"Internal trauma?"

"Yes."

Now his breathing wasn't nearly as steady, either. "Nerve damage?"

A brief pause. "Yes."

Stellar light. How invincible was she? "Is there anything you can't heal?"

A longer pause. "I don't know."

Well, at least she was being completely honest. "What about other people? Can you heal all their injuries, too?" Because if she could, he'd have to question why she was hiding out in a cabin in the woods. Her abilities could make a huge difference in a hospital emergency room. He'd seen what she'd done with Paul Bunyan. At least one of his fingers had looked broken until she'd engaged her field around him.

"That's much harder."

"How much harder?"

"A lot harder." She slid her fingers free from his and rotated her wrist so her palm showed. "And it depends on where the injury is located. Hands are easiest, because of the energy centers there." She spread her fingers, then formed a loose fist.

That tracked with what he knew about energy healing. But what she was describing was still leaps and bounds above anything he'd heard of before.

"New injuries are easier, too."

That was the first piece of information she'd volunteered. And another twinge of guilt in her emotional field brought him back to the first time he'd seen her, right after the plane crash. She'd been glowing then, too. "New injuries. Like after my plane hit your shield and the tree? How badly was I injured?"

Her pain and guilt spiked, giving him his answer even before she spoke.

"You were... hurt."

Hurt. The word didn't tell him much, but her emotions made it clear anyone else would have rushed him to a hospital. He'd woken up in her bed, instead. "You healed me." Not really a question.

More guilt. And a long pause. "Not exactly."

Not exactly? Then what... His mind filled in the gaps, pulling in other clues from the past two days. "It was Marina." He remembered the glimpse of her emerald green energy field, the cooling touch as she'd taken away the burning in his eyes, Gryphon's comments that she had a medical background.

A slow nod. "She's a very powerful healer. Much stronger than me."

The room was starting to spin. "Can she produce a stronger shield, too?"

"No. That's not a gift of the Ne—" She cut off. "She can't shield."

She'd used the word gift. "She was born with healing abilities?" He'd assumed their energy talents were the result of extensive training.

Her anxiety was climbing again. And she didn't answer.

She didn't need to. If Marina had been born with energy abilities, he'd be willing to bet Libra had been born with her abilities, too. Everything she was saying illustrated she and Marina represented a huge leap forward in human evolution.

But her entire life was designed to hide that fact. He didn't understand why, and maybe he didn't need to, at least not tonight.

She was too kindhearted and compassionate to not have good reasons. Pushing her any further would only add to her emotional overload.

Sighing, he rested his cheek against her hair. "I know you're worried. I can feel it. And I know you and Marina must have reasons for keeping your abilities secret. I respect that."

Some of the tension eased from her shoulders

"I just hope you believe that I would never do anything to hurt you. Or Marina. Whatever you tell me, stays with me. I promise."

Her anxiety slowly ebbed, her breathing smoothing out. "I've never talked to anyone about this before."

That he could easily believe.

"We can't share the truth about our abilities with others. It wouldn't be... safe."

Not safe. That kicked off a new set of mental images. His grip around her waist tightened. "You think people would come after you if they found out?" That thought hadn't occurred to him until now, but she might be right. Abilities like hers would be coveted.

"Yes."

What a terrifying thought. At least she'd proven she could defend herself if she had to. But their quiet, secluded lifestyle was starting to make a whole lot more sense.

Unfortunately, his lifestyle was anything but quiet and secluded. Finding a way to make her a part of it might be a bigger mountain to climb than he'd imagined.

Twenty-Six

Libra had wrestled with herself during the walk to the B&B, planning out what she was going to say. And what she wasn't.

But it hadn't gone as she'd thought it would. Brendan hadn't reacted with fear. Or judgment. Which had opened the door to sharing far more than she'd expected to. Saying anything about Marina was an added risk, but one she'd needed to take. Instinct told her she could trust him. And she wanted to. Oh, how she wanted to.

Talking about her abilities, giving him a glimpse into who she was behind the façade, was thrilling and terrifying. So far, he'd shown amazing composure and acceptance. Which kept the flame of hope burning. She'd been so afraid the dream of a potential future together had guttered and died after he'd seen what she could do.

But he was still here. Holding her. Trusting her. Loving her.

Her gaze drifted to the bed. They'd come here to join in a physical bond that would echo their emotional bond. Did he still want that? Could the night still end with pleasure and joy?

Turning her head, she nuzzled his neck, testing the waters. "Can we talk about something else?"

His breath caught, his chest rising and falling more rapidly.

A promising reaction. She flicked out her tongue, tasting the slightly salty flavor of his skin.

His arms tightened around her. "What do you want to talk about?"

He might have been trying to sound casual, but he failed miserably.

"You." She continued her exploration to his earlobe, shifting position so she could catch the tender flesh between her teeth.

His fingers splayed across her lower back, pressing her close. "What do you want to know?"

Using her tongue, she traced the curve of his ear. He shuddered in response. "I want to know how this makes you feel," she whispered.

With a groan he turned his head, capturing her mouth in a kiss that burned a line straight to her core. Question answered.

"It makes me feel like that," he growled.

She gripped his shoulders, pulling him closer.

He came willingly, and kept moving, pushing off the couch and taking her with him. As soon as they were upright his mouth found hers again, his tongue delving deep as his hands settled her hips firmly against his.

An arrow of pleasure struck as she made contact with the hard length underneath the fabric separating them. She pressed against him and was rewarded with another flash of pleasure that triggered her energy field. It flared around them, heightening the sensations at every point of contact.

He held her tighter and rocked forward, their moans mingling. He broke the kiss, breathing hard. "This isn't how I'd planned things to go."

Her hands moved to the front of his shirt, fumbling with the buttons. "What did you... plan?" She wanted the shirt off now, but the buttons wouldn't give under her trembling fingers. Grasping the lapels, she yanked, popping the buttons off and exposing his bare chest to the touch of her hands and energy field.

His harsh inhalation was her only warning before she became weightless. The room spun, and then she was cradled between the soft caress of the comforter and the hard press of his muscled body.

"It would be slow." The fire burning in his blue eyes set her ablaze as he wrenched off his shirt and tossed it away. "Tender." His lips met hers, his kiss the opposite of his words as his tongue stroked with deliberate intent and his hands shoved up the fabric of her skirt. "Romantic." His palms glided along the skin of her thighs to the furnace heating her from the inside out.

His hand pulled on the fabric of her panties, removing the thin barrier. She gasped as his fingers caressed her with firm assurance. Her hips bucked, her body taking control of her reaction.

"Yes," he purred against her mouth, his tongue mimicking the movements of his fingers as he buried them inside. "That's it."

Her hips bucked again, his finger stroking a point that blasted all rational thought from her mind. Her body tightened around his fingers, her thighs quivering as he continued to drive her forward.

"Come for me, Libra. *Now*."

Her body obeyed his command, a wave of pleasure washing over her as her energy field pulsed in time to the contractions.

He stayed with her as her body arched off the mattress, supporting her as the ripples continued, slowly easing her down from the peak. "Yes." Sliding off the bed, he stripped off his pants with jerky movements. The lamplight on his skin revealed the work of art she knew she would find, complete with a generous and proud erection.

He pulled a small packet out of the pocket of his pants, knelt on the bed beside her, and tore the packet open.

"What's that?"

He paused, holding the circular object in his hand as his gaze met hers. "What?"

She pointed at the object. "That?"

He looked at the object, then at her. "The condom?"

"Oh. Condom." She'd heard the term, but never seen one.

He stared at her with a strange look on his face. "Have you... is this your first time using a condom?"

"Yes." The Suulh had no need for them. She and Brendan didn't need them either, but she couldn't explain why without revealing her alien origins. She wasn't ready for that.

He sat back on his heels. "Libra, is this your first time having sex?"

His hesitancy puzzled her. "Yes."

He looked away and muttered a word she didn't know.

"Is that a problem?"

"Problem?" He met her gaze. "I've been acting like a randy teenager while dealing with a virgin. So, yeah, that's a problem."

The only problem she saw was that his erection was fading. "Why? Don't I please you?"

He barked out a laugh, shaking his head. "Everything you do pleases me."

He wasn't making sense. "Then why—"

"That's part of the problem, too. The moment you touch me I lose all reason, especially when you get assertive. I was about two seconds away from going all in without realizing what that would mean for you."

"It would mean pleasure." She stroked a finger along his thigh. "Great pleasure."

His gaze softened, the tenderness he'd spoken of earlier now taking command. "Not necessarily the first time, at least for you. It can be a bit painful."

She shook her head. "You can't hurt me."

"You may think that, but—"

Enough talking. She wanted him. Now.

Reaching out, she grasped his firm length in her hand.

He jerked, his eyes widening as he stared at where she held him.

But that wasn't the reaction she wanted. Rising onto her knees, she engaged her energy field. Sure enough, the skin beneath her fingers swelled.

He swallowed hard. "Libra—"

She cut him off with a kiss, running her thumb along the ridge of his growing erection.

His body shook, a groan rumbling out of his chest.

Much better. She ended the kiss, looking deeply into his eyes. "You can't hurt me."

Understanding finally dawned. "Because of your energy field?"

She nodded. Her field was part of being Suulh, so in a way, it *was* the reason. Just not the whole reason.

He took a shuddering breath. "You're sure?"

"Positive."

"Okay." The corners of his mouth curved. "But I still want to take it slow."

She scowled.

He chuckled. "Don't worry. If your reaction last time is any indication, I won't be able to hold out for long." His gaze dropped to where she gripped him. "That is, if you'll let me go."

She acquiesced. He was almost as hard now as he'd been before her question had derailed them. *Note to self. Don't ask questions during sex.*

Reaching past her, he pulled the comforter back. "I have a fantasy of seeing you naked, stretched out on this bed." He looked pointedly at the dress she was still wearing. "Will you give me that visual?"

As if he had to ask. Grabbing the hem of the dress, she slipped it off her body and over her head, dropping it on the floor beside the bed. Her bra quickly followed.

His soft groan was rewarding, as was the heat burning in his eyes. The sheets felt cool on her fevered skin as she pressed back into them. "Is this what you wanted?"

He gripped the footboard with one hand, the condom with the other. "You have no idea." He rolled the condom on with brisk efficiency before prowling toward her on his hands and knees. "You are my every fantasy come true."

And he was a fantasy she hadn't even dared to dream. She held out her arms. "Then love me."

A different light glowed in his eyes. "Oh, I intend to."

Twenty-Seven

Brendan couldn't imagine this night getting any stranger, but at the moment, he didn't care. The most beautiful woman he'd ever known was stretched out beneath him, the scent of her desire tantalizing him and the depth of her emotions stroking his empathic senses.

Bracing on his forearms, he gazed into eyes the color of the ocean in Hawaii, surrounded by a pearlescent glow that filled him with joy. "You are magical."

"I am yours."

His throat constricted. *Please let that be true.* They had so much still to learn about each other, so many questions unanswered, but he knew this moment would be burned into his brain for the rest of his life.

Settling his hips between the juncture of her thighs, he probed gently, her heat calling to him. Thanks to his empathic senses, he'd know if he was causing her pain, and could slow things down.

Or that was his plan. Libra threw it out the window when she gripped his glutes, lifted her hips, and took him all the way to the hilt in one firm motion.

Sensation shot through him like a locomotive, the power of it driving the air from his lungs on a muttered oath.

She stilled. "Was that wrong?"

He squeezed his eyes shut and gritted his teeth, fighting the overwhelming urge to come. "No. You just..." He inhaled through his nose in short pants as her energy field continued to caress him. "Took me... by surprise."

"I wanted to feel this."

Her core muscles contracted, making him hiss. "Careful." He was so close. Too damn close.

"Are you okay?"

He took another steadying breath before risking a peek at her.

She was gazing at him with concern. That's when he clued into the emotions his empathic senses were sending him. She was worried. But not in any pain. She'd been right about that.

Her worry gave him something to focus on, easing him away from the precipice. "Just trying not to come."

"Come? You mean release?"

He smiled, though to her it probably looked more primal. "Yes, release."

"You could release right now?" Far from being upset, she seemed delighted.

"I could. But I don't want to. Not yet."

"Why not?"

If he'd had any doubts about her virgin status, her comment proved she'd never had sex before. "Because it's a lot more pleasurable if you draw it out." And this conversation was helping him achieve that, though he still felt like a rocket on final countdown.

"Oh." An impish light lit her eyes. "So, what do we do now?"

"That depends. I'm going to try moving a bit." He slid out halfway and drove back in. And swore. It was just that good.

"*Oh!*"

His empathic senses telegraphed her pleasure at the same time the exhalation left her lips. And he was right back where he'd started, ready to go off after one thrust.

Then she gripped her core muscles again, and he lost the thread of his control.

"I'm sorry, I can't..." He couldn't even finish the sentence. Lifting onto his forearms, he slid back and pumped into her, stroke after stroke sending a blast of combined pleasure that sparked through every cell in his body.

It should have ended quickly, but instead the pressure kept building, the intensity shattering all thought and throwing him into a whirlpool of sensation with Libra at the center. She cried out his name, her body pulsing around him in a shimmering glow, drawing him with her as they hurtled over the edge together in a climax that exploded his world like a supernova.

The room disappeared, all thoughts of his surroundings blasted away. There was only Libra, their connection fusing them together for all time.

Her joy wrapped around him like a cocoon, her energy field intensifying the feeling of joining. He'd never known this type of soul-deep bonding was possible. Libra's emotions felt like an extension of himself, a direct line that he knew on some level she could sense, too.

Which is why he wasn't sure which of them started laughing first. It wasn't funny laughter, but rather an effervescent happiness that couldn't be contained.

Lifting his head, he gazed into her eyes, his deep chuckle playing tag with her higher-pitched giggle. "Well, that was fun."

She grinned. "Lots of fun."

Dipping down, he brushed his lips across hers. "I told you the next time I'd release."

She caught his bottom lip between her teeth, running her tongue along the sensitive skin before letting go. "You were right."

And just like that, he was ready for round two. "And I'm going to prove it to you again right now."

"Oh?"

He slid his steadily expanding erection out of her warm channel. "I just need to fetch another condom and dispose of this one."

She caught his arm with her hand. "You don't need another one."

He stilled, his mind going on high alert. "Why not?"

Her laughter had disappeared, replaced by a flicker of anxiety. "I can't contract or transmit disease. And I can't become pregnant."

Bam! His stomach bottomed out, the pain of loss taking him down at the knees. He sank back on his heels. "You're sterile?" He hadn't realized until that moment how much children had been part of his dream with her.

She frowned. "Sterile?"

"You can't have children," he clarified.

The frown faded. "Of course I can have children. But it will be a conscious choice, not an accident."

Now he was the one frowning. "So, you're using some kind of contraception?"

Her lips pursed. "I won't conceive unless I choose to."

He was missing something. He could feel it. Something important. "Does this have something to do with your energy abilities?"

"Yes. I control my fertility."

If another woman had claimed such a thing, he never would have accepted it at face value. He didn't take the possibility of creating a child lightly. But Libra wasn't just another woman. Her abilities were pushing the boundaries of his experience every second. And, perhaps more important, creating a child with her had become one of his life goals. If it happened tonight, he wouldn't regret it for a second.

He also didn't doubt her claim about disease. Not after what he'd witnessed tonight, and what she'd told him. Even if he didn't have that first-hand knowledge, he'd believe her. She had secrets, more than most, but he knew without a doubt she would never do anything to intentionally harm him.

Which put him in an extremely unusual position. He'd never had sex without a condom.

Slipping off the bed, he stood. "I'll be right back."

He disposed of the condom in the bathroom, then snagged a washcloth off the rack and took a moment to give his good buddy a quick washdown. When the main event started, he wanted to be clean. The warm water combined with the visions his mind was generating had a predictable effect, restoring his erection to the fully upright and locked position. It also gave him another idea.

Grabbing a second washcloth, he ran it under the warm water and wrung it out, then pulled one of the hand towels off the rack and carried them both into the bedroom.

He stopped and stared, captivated by the image of Libra stretched out on the bed, propped on one elbow facing him, her head on her palm.

Her gaze flicked to the washcloth. "Is that for me?"

He had to clear his throat before he could answer. "It is if you're interested."

Desire glowed in her eyes. "Oh, I'm interested."

That got him moving. He knelt on the bed, laying the hand towel beside her. "I'd be delighted if you'd let me do the honors."

Her response sucked all the moisture from his mouth as she rolled onto her back and spread her thighs. "Be my guest."

His hand shook as he crouched beside her. *Keep it together, buddy.* Easy to say, but he'd never been with a woman as potent as Libra. Everything she said, everything she did ramped him up, like her energy abilities were overloading his systems.

Not that he was complaining. He'd happily short-circuit a few fuses for the gift of loving her.

Dipping the washcloth down, he stroked it along her silken thigh, starting at her knee and working steadily higher. Her hips shifted and her breathing changed as he switched to the other thigh, giving it the same loving attention as the first.

On impulse, he leaned down and blew across the damp skin. Her hips rose in response.

Oh, yeah. This was going to work out *very* well.

The scent of her desire grew as he reached her core. The first touch of the cloth to her swollen flesh produced a shudder through her petite frame and a moan that made his erection twitch. He tried a lighter touch, brushing back and forth across the tender skin. Her fingers curled into the sheets as she started to pant.

Leaning down, he blew air across the same point.

Her back arched, thrusting her plump breasts up, reminding him he hadn't explored that territory, yet.

Trailing the washcloth along her abdomen to her ribcage, he dragged it across her left nipple.

She gasped, her hand latching onto his arm. "Brendan, please."

He had a feeling she didn't even know what she was asking for, but he did. Lowering his head, he took the ripe peak into his mouth.

Her energy field flared, enveloping him and pulsing against his skin in time to the suction he applied to her breast. He moved over her, caging her in with his arms as he feasted on her other breast, her energy field and his empathic senses transmitting each pull of his mouth and each nip of his teeth on her flesh straight to his erection. He'd never experienced something so erotic in his life.

Her hips lifted, brushing the stiff ridge of his erection.

She moaned.

So did he.

Leaving the bounty of her breasts he slid higher, capturing her mouth in a searing kiss as he lowered his hips to hers and found her entrance. With one firm thrust, he shot home.

Her cry blended with his, their tongues tangling as he began a steady rhythm. He couldn't process the sensation of being inside her— no barriers, fully connected. He felt... everything.

She gripped the back of his head, devouring his mouth as her hips rose in time with each thrust, sending shockwave after shockwave through his body.

Never like this. Never like this. Never...

And then she came, her muscles contracting around him in an iron grip as her muffled cry filled his mouth. Her reaction tore a release from his body that roared like an inferno, making his ears ring and his heart stutter as he drove into her again and again and again.

Libra! Libra! Libra!

The final surge toppled him. He dragged her with him, pulling her onto her side, their bodies still fused together as he sank into oblivion.

Twenty-Eight

Marina had lied to her.

Or at least downplayed the truth.

When Libra saw her in the morning, they were going to have a good long talk. Nothing her friend had told her had prepared her for what it would feel like to experience sex with Brendan.

Yes, Marina had made it sound pleasurable. And fun.

But this! She had no words. She'd felt like she was walking through a lava field that burned her to the core, but with pleasure, not pain. This joining, this elemental connection, had taken possession of her body, her mind, her soul.

Even now, as she lay beside Brendan, watching the steady rise and fall of his chest, she felt bound to him in a way she couldn't define. She also felt stronger. Calmer. More focused than she could ever remember feeling.

Their sexual joining had done that. And she'd had no idea it was even possible.

His eyelids fluttered, then lifted, his gaze focusing on her face as a slow smile curved his lips. "Hey, there."

"Hi. You dozed off."

His smile grew. "So I see." His arm tightened around her. "You pack a punch."

She wasn't entirely certain what he meant, but it sounded like a compliment. "Thank you."

He laughed. "You're welcome." His gaze drifted down the length of their bodies to where they were still joined. "Guess I didn't want to leave the party."

"Neither did I."

His gaze met hers. "That's good to hear."

"Is it always like this?"

"Sex?"

She nodded.

"No. This was... extraordinary."

So he'd never experienced this with a Human female. That pleased her, and gave even more credence to Marina's belief that they could be mates in every sense of the word. "Do you think it will always be like this for us?"

A warm glow that had nothing to do with sex lit his eyes. "I do."

She bathed in that glow, and the promise it held. "Do you want children?"

He barked out a laugh. "You are direct, aren't you?" He grinned at her, nudging his hips against hers. "Oh yeah, I want children. Do you?"

"Of course. My daughter and Lelindia will be... close."

"Daughter, huh?" He stroked his fingers down her cheek and across her lips. "I'm sure she'll be as beautiful as her mother. And Lelindia will be thrilled."

Her mouth tingled from his touch. "Yes." Her daughter might not be as powerful as she could be with a Suulh father, but she no longer cared. Now that she'd experienced this physical joining with Brendan, she couldn't imagine sharing this form of bonding with anyone else.

He continued the light caress. "Just to be clear, you are asking if I want to be the father of this hypothetical daughter, right?"

"Yes." Although there was nothing hypothetical about it. Marina hadn't put a fine point on it, but she must have evaluated Brendan's physical state before she'd even brought up the idea of a potential mating. She would have confirmed he was capable of producing a child.

He sighed, a contented, happy hum. Cupping her jaw, he kissed her with a reverence that drew an answering sigh from her lips.

"I love you, Libra," he murmured, his lips hovering over hers. But rather than touching down again, he held perfectly still, as if waiting for her reaction.

Which reminded her she was supposed to respond. For the Suulh, words didn't have the importance that they held for Humans. An energetic connection said so much more. But Brendan wouldn't understand that, or what the glow of her energy field during sex meant for her, or their future as mates. But he would, soon. "I love you, Brendan."

Right answer. Rolling her to her back, he kissed her again. His tongue caressed hers in tender strokes, without the intensity or heat he'd shown before. This felt more intimate, more sensual.

She opened to him, spreading her thighs as he moved within her, the slow glide of his erection creating an entirely new sensation than his firm thrusts. She reveled in it, her body growing liquid beneath his, catching his easy rhythm.

He lifted his mouth from hers, meeting her gaze as he continued to stroke into her. "How soon were you thinking of conceiving our daughter?"

A humming sound rose from her throat as he shifted the angle, touching off a new point of pleasure. "After the mating ceremony."

"Mating ceremony?" His breath was coming in shorter bursts now. "You mean wedding?"

"Wedding, yes." She'd never seen one, never imagined they would be relevant to her, but from what she'd heard, it was a more formal and wordy version of a Suulh mating ceremony.

His tempo slowed, his gaze firmly locked on hers. "Did you just ask me to marry you?"

Marry? Wasn't that the same thing as a wedding? The friction between their bodies was generating all kinds of wonderful sensations, making it tough to focus. "Yes. To become a mated pair."

He stilled, the look in his eyes generating almost as much pleasure as his touch. "Then yes, I would love to marry you, and conceive our daughter."

She stared at him for a heartbeat, the reality sinking in. When it hit her center, her energy field responded, enveloping them both in an embrace of sensual joy that startled a gasp from her chest and lifted her hips.

His eyes widened, his hips locking against hers, triggering answering spasms from her core. "Oh, Libra," he groaned, pressing tighter as his body trembled in sync with hers.

The waves of pleasure rolled on and on, each pulse of her field drawing breathless cries from their lips.

When it finally ended, Brendan slumped beside her, one arm and leg draped over her body. "Incredible," he murmured, his voice thick.

"Mmm." She couldn't even manage a coherent word. Her body had gone boneless. But a giddy happiness bubbled in her chest.

She'd found her mate. Brendan had triggered her energy field and awoken her heart.

Together, they would produce the next Sahzade, building a future filled with passion and joy unlike anything she'd ever known.

Twenty-Nine

Brendan gave himself lots of bonus points for getting Libra to the farmers market on time.

It hadn't been easy. When his alarm went off, Libra's back had been pressed against his chest, her delightful tush aligned with his hips. It had taken his mind exactly two seconds to conjure an image of one of the many delights he and Libra hadn't experienced yet. But he hadn't trusted himself to stick to the timetable, which is also why he'd taken a cold shower—alone—rather than suggest Libra join him for a very hot one.

But he had a heck of a consolation prize. Libra was going to marry him. They'd have the rest of their lives to share sensual pleasure.

He still couldn't quite believe it, even as they rode in the transport to the market, her hand in his and her head snuggled against his shoulder. Not only did she want to marry him, she wanted to conceive a child right away. That had caught him by surprise, as had her pronouncement that they'd have a daughter.

Maybe she was right. For all he knew daughters ran in her family. He'd have to get her to open up about her past if he wanted to find out. And he'd love a daughter, a little Libra with her mother's spirit and abilities. She could be a playmate for Lelindia whenever they were together.

And how often will that be?

He tried to ignore the nagging voice in his head, but it had grown steadily louder ever since they'd left the cozy isolation of the B&B. He still hadn't told her about his company. They also hadn't discussed how marrying him would alter the life she'd built here. Last night those topics hadn't been a blip on his radar. Now they were building like a tropical storm.

His dad hadn't faced this problem. His mom had known who he was from the beginning. And their high-profile lifestyles had complimented each other.

His and Libra's lives were polar opposites. Once he completed his doctorate and took the reins of the company full-time, he'd spend as much time off-world as he did at his house on Oahu, maybe more. His parents certainly had, and he'd loved being part of their adventures.

But Libra had built her life around seclusion and secrecy, wanting to prevent anyone from finding out about her abilities. Considering how limited her resources were, he could see why that choice had made sense to her. She would have been vulnerable, but his wealth and connections could protect her. He might even be able to find a way for her to make use of her skills in a productive, safe environment, something she wasn't likely to achieve on her own.

He could offer the same to Marina and Gryphon, which would be the elegant solution. Then they could all stay together.

"We're here."

Libra scooted over to the door.

He hadn't even realized the transport had stopped.

He followed her out onto the packed dirt parking area, snagging their bags from the transport's trunk.

Several larger vehicles sat in the lot, including Gryphon's. A converted barn took up the rest of the space. Colorful signs fluttered in the breeze though most of the exterior enclosures were empty. During the warmer months, that probably changed.

He walked with Libra through the wide doorway at one end. Vendors bustled around inside, setting up tables and displays, carrying in crates and bins. He spotted Gryphon about a fourth of the way down the row, his height making him easy to see.

But it was Lelindia who noticed them first. With a high-pitched squeal, she raced down the aisle, barely slowing as she smacked into their legs and wrapped her arms as far around their waists as she could in a group hug. "Hi!"

He'd braced for impact, having experienced her preferred greeting before. "Hi!" Shifting their bags to one hand he crouched so they were on eye level. "How have you been?"

"Great! We're settin' up."

He grinned. "Then put us to work."

"Okay!" Grabbing his free hand and one of Libra's, she tugged them to where Gryphon and Marina were waiting.

"I see she found you," Gryphon called out, his grin matching Brendan's.

"Yep. No hiding from this one." He nodded toward the tables, where the boxes filled with Libra's decorative items and the display banners sat. "How can I help?"

"Libra and Marina handle the setup, so why don't you come with me to fetch the food bins and stow your bags?"

"Sounds good." He gave Lelindia's hand a squeeze. "I'll be back."

"Okay." She bounded over to her mother.

He glanced at Libra, who was already moving toward one of the tables. She gave him a secret smile that revved his engines, his thoughts drifting back to the adult activities they'd enjoyed last night.

Turning, he followed Gryphon as he headed in the direction they'd come, weaving through the vendors setting up in the open stalls.

Gryphon shortened his ground-eating stride as they exited the building. "I take it things went well last night?"

"You could say that." Other than the mean drunk who'd tried to slice his throat and the difficult conversation with Libra that had followed. But the rest of the evening had been pure bliss. "We're getting married."

Gryphon paused with one hand on the back hatch of his vehicle. He turned his head in slow motion. "Is that so?"

He'd prepared for the emotional shift. Sure enough, Gryphon had gone from light and breezy to focused and cautious.

"It was her idea." Damn. He sounded defensive.

"Kinda fast."

"I know." And with Gryphon staring at him like a disapproving parent, he was starting to question their impulsiveness. "It was a really intense night."

"Good sex?"

The direct question startled a nervous laugh out of him. "Um, yeah." Best of his life. Maybe the best in the history of sex. He glanced over his shoulder, confirming they were alone. "I found out about her shield."

Gryphon's mouth popped open in surprise. "She told you?"

"She sort of had to." He gave Gryphon a short summary of their encounter with the drunk. "She saved my life."

The look in Gryphon's eyes changed, keeping pace with the shift in his emotions, caution and doubt replaced by a solemn acceptance. "She's chosen her mate," he murmured, barely loud enough for Brendan to hear.

"We chose each other. I want to be with her more than anything."

"Anything?" Doubt infused the word. "Have you told her about your life? About what her future would look like after you're mated?"

He shifted uncomfortably. Gryphon had tapped on a pressure point. "No. But I can offer her anything she needs, anything she wants. She won't have to live in fear."

"Hmm." Gryphon turned back to the vehicle, opening the door and hauling out a couple bins. After setting up a collapsible rolling cart, he started handing bins to Brendan to stack on the cart. "She hasn't told you about her past, has she?"

"Not yet. I know it's a painful subject. But we'll get there. And I'll help her through it."

The look Gryphon shot him wasn't encouraging. Neither was his heartfelt sigh. "Boy, you don't have any idea the battle you're wading into. Being with Libra will change your world." He lifted the last bin and set it on the cart before closing up the vehicle. "Make sure you're willing to sacrifice who you are for who you'll become. Otherwise, you should hop the next train out of town and never look back."

Well, that was depressing.

He pondered Gryphon's words as they walked back into the building. What did he mean, *sacrifice who you are*? Was it a warning? Was he implying Libra would refuse to leave the cabin, to move beyond this town, this simple life, even after she discovered the galaxy of opportunities he could offer her? But why? Especially after he made it clear he'd gladly take all four of them as a package deal.

He hadn't said anything about that to Gryphon. He should have. Gryphon was probably concerned about the fallout if he tried to take Libra away from him and Marina. Libra would definitely object to that. But he'd never ask her to make that choice.

Once they were back at the cabin, he'd clarify that point with everyone.

It didn't take long before he was caught up in the lively activity of the market, pushing his concerns to the back of his mind. Gryphon was a born salesman, calling out to folks as they passed, engaging them in conversation, swapping stories and recipe ideas with the regulars. Marina wasn't as boisterous, but she handled most of the questions regarding the produce and seedlings they had available for purchase. Brendan helped Libra process the transactions and restock the displays, which gave him an excuse to touch her hand or brush against her shoulder or hip on a regular basis. Maybe not the smartest move, considering how it affected him, but he didn't stop.

And she clearly didn't want him to. Every time they touched, he felt her zing of pleasure, and flare of heat. He'd also caught her watching him whenever she wasn't helping a customer, a glow in her turquoise eyes that beckoned him closer.

Lelindia was his fail safe. She spent most of her time with him or Libra, although occasionally she'd skip out into the crowd and draw people over to the booth with the same enthusiasm her dad showed. It didn't take much imagination for him to picture her a few years older, with a blonde-haired little girl skipping by her side.

His and Libra's daughter.

That thought pulled him like a magnet to Libra. He slipped his arm around her shoulders and gave her a quick hug, his only option with the line of customers waiting. Her emotional response warmed his heart, and got him thinking about how they'd handle sleeping arrangements going forward. He couldn't imagine staying on the couch, not with Libra in the next room. He also couldn't imagine her wanting him to. Why stay apart when they could be together in her bed? Hopefully Gryphon and Marina wouldn't throw up any objections.

By the time the market wound down, the tables were almost bare, and his feet were a little sore. He wasn't used to standing for hours on end.

He helped Gryphon restack the bins while Libra and Marina disassembled the displays and took down the banners.

"Did you like it?" Lelindia asked him, hopping on her toes beside him.

Where did she get all the energy? He was exhausted, but she practically glowed with enthusiasm. "Sure did, firefly! You and your dad know how to work the crowd."

Her petite brows pulled down in a small frown. "Work the crowd?"

"He means we're good at talking to people." Gryphon scooped her off the ground and planted a kiss on her cheek. "We make a good team."

She wrapped her arms around his neck and snuggled cheek-to-cheek. "Good team."

The image shot right to Brendan's heart. He wanted that for himself. A daughter to love and cherish, to laugh and joke with.

Libra seemed to believe it was a certainty. He hoped she was right.

Thirty

Watching Brendan at the market had brought clarity to Libra's visions of their future. He fit in so well, joking with Gryphon, talking with Marina, playing with Lelindia. It was so easy, effortless, like he'd been with them for years, not days.

She suspected he'd said something to Gryphon about their plans to mate. Gryphon's mood had changed when they'd returned. That was fine. She'd told Marina, too, although with the other vendors nearby she hadn't been able to share any details. Marina had been surprised, but mostly positive.

She also hadn't been able to get Marina's counsel on how to broach the subject of her non-Human heritage. She didn't think Brendan would react badly. He'd handled her revelations about her shield and healing abilities well last night.

But thinking about it still made her tummy clench. She'd never told anyone her secret before. It was a huge step, one she needed to take before they were mated. Brendan deserved no less.

He held her hand on the drive back to the cabin. Lelindia sat on his other side and kept up a lively commentary, pointing out all the varieties of trees, shrubs, and ground cover they passed on the way. Brendan was an attentive listener, which encouraged Lelindia's natural enthusiasm. He was the first person the little Nedale had spent any time with who didn't know as much about plants as she did, and she was soaking up his attention like a sunflower at midday.

Unpacking the transport and returning the bins to the greenhouse didn't take long with all five of them pitching in.

"I baked bread last night for sandwiches," Gryphon informed Brendan. "I make a mean grilled veggie if you're interested."

Brendan grinned. "Are you twisting my arm?"

"You bet. I'll give you another cooking lesson in the process."

While they headed into the kitchen with Lelindia right behind them, Libra followed Marina to the middle bedroom, swinging the door shut behind her.

Marina turned, not looking the least bit surprised by her presence.

"I need your advice."

Marina's gaze flicked in the direction of the closed door. "About whether to tell Brendan the truth?"

There were advantages to having a friend who could read you like a book. "Yes. I can't mate with him while he still believes I'm Human. It wouldn't be fair. But telling him will affect you and Gryphon, too."

"As will mating with him. It's only been a few days. I know I nudged you in that direction, but I didn't expect you to decide so quickly."

"Neither did I." The clatter of pans drifted through the thick wood of the door. She lowered her voice. "But I can't imagine being with anyone else. It was so much more than I'd expected. So much more than you'd told me."

Marina smiled at the rebuke. "I'll admit I downplayed the potential for connection when I thought you would mate with Wolf. It didn't seem likely he would trigger your field. I didn't want you to be disappointed."

Remembered pleasure spread warmth through her body. "I wasn't disappointed."

"I should hope not, considering you plan to mate with him. And I assume, conceive the next Sahzade?"

Libra nodded. The urge to bear that child was growing stronger by the hour.

Marina settled onto the edge of the bed and patted the space beside her.

Libra sat, the familiar sensation of Marina's nearness soothing the rough edges of her emotions.

"So tell me, was he accepting of the intimacy of your energy field during sex?"

Accepting wasn't the word she'd use. "He loved it."

"That's a good sign. Have you told him anything about the extent of your abilities? Or why you have them?"

"I had to last night." She filled Marina in on what had occurred at the restaurant and then on the street afterward.

Marina's eyes widened and her brows lifted as the story progressed. "He watched you shield and didn't demand an explanation? Or pull away emotionally?"

She shook her head. "I thought for sure I'd ruined everything between us, but he wanted to talk about it, learn more about what I could do."

"Wow. That's... an unusual reaction." Marina gazed at her for a moment. "How did you explain your shielding ability without telling him you weren't Human?"

She fidgeted. "I didn't really explain it. We talked more about healing than the shield. And about you. He knows you're a stronger healer than I am, and that you can't produce a shield."

"And he didn't question why you and I have those abilities?"

"He asked if you were born with them. I didn't answer."

"Hmm. So, you evaded."

"Yes." Evading was all she'd ever known, at least since she was a child. Having an honest, open discussion about who she was, where she came from, what she could do, wasn't something she'd ever faced.

"And you're certain you want to tell him the truth? It sounds like so far he's accepted everything as extraordinary, but still without the realm of Human experience. You could let him keep believing that."

"I guess so." Except she didn't want to. Hiding the truth from Brendan would feel like a betrayal, one that would cut deeper the longer they were together. Even now guilt and anxiety were gnawing at her. "But then we'd never have what you and Gryphon share. I'd always be holding part of myself back. Hiding."

She didn't want to hide from Brendan. She wanted to throw open the doors and let his warm light chase away the darkness of her past. "I wouldn't be able to be completely myself with my daughter, either."

"True." Marina gazed out the window at the trees, but Libra doubted she was seeing them. A sigh slipped from Marina's lips as she turned back. "It's not an easy decision, but it's yours to make, Sahzade. You know I will support you."

Yes, that she knew with absolute certainty.

Their world had been destroyed, the future of their race lost to the cosmos, but Marina was still the Nedale, and she was still the Sahzade, the leader of the Suulh. Their traditions gave her the final word on all matters pertaining to the well-being of their people. Marina might argue with her, but she wouldn't defy her when she'd made a decision, even if she disagreed. Marina's unwavering support was the only constant in her life. "How do I tell him? What do I say?"

"I'd suggest being blunt. Eliminate all risk of confusion or misunderstanding. Say something like *the reason I have energy abilities is because I'm not Human. I come from a planet far from Earth.*"

Just hearing the words from Marina's mouth set her heart pounding. "That certainly wouldn't leave any room for doubt."

"No, it wouldn't."

Which was what she wanted, right? To be accepted for who she really was? To be able to build a life with him that was as full and rich as what Marina and Gryphon shared? No secrets. No fear.

Well, except for the fear twining around her heart right now. The only way she could clear it was to place her trust in Brendan, to say what needed to be said. "Okay. After lunch we'll go out to the greenhouse and... talk."

"Are you sure you want to do it alone? We could all discuss it here."

The offer gave her pause, reminding her of the repercussions of her actions. But a group meeting felt wrong. "I think it would be easier for him to hear if it's just the two of us. It would give him time to process and react without being watched."

"It might be harder for you, though."

"Maybe." Her concern was appreciated, but if ever there was a time for her to stand firmly on her own two feet, this was it. "I can handle it."

"I know you can." Marina slid an arm around her shoulders and squeezed. "I hope he understands what a gift you're giving him."

"I think he will." He'd certainly cherished her last night. Those memories, and her dreams for their mating, would give her the courage she'd need to face the obstacles before her. Their future was worth fighting for.

Thirty-One

Gryphon's cooking lesson, and Lelindia's energetic presence, kept Brendan occupied after they returned to the cabin, but it didn't prevent him from sensing Libra's fluctuating emotions, and Marina's concern. It reminded him of how he'd felt while talking to Gryphon at the market.

He didn't blame Gryphon and Marina for being anxious. He barely recognized himself these days. Impulsiveness wasn't a trait he normally exhibited, but ever since Libra had slammed into his life in a burst of light, he couldn't resist the magnetic pull drawing them together.

And if he was completely honest, he didn't want to. What he did want was more information about her past, and her family. If he was right that she and Marina had inherited their energy abilities, knowing more about their histories would help explain what they could do. Or at least he hoped it would. It would definitely give him a better idea of how he could help Libra going forward.

But first he needed to explain his own situation, let her know how much being together would ease the burdens she was carrying. Whether she chose to make her abilities known to the public or not, he could insure she didn't have to fear that someone would take advantage of her or manipulate her. He could also introduce her to the top minds in metaphysics and parapsychology. They would be thrilled to talk to her and Marina, to work with them to explore the full potential of their talents.

About the time the sandwiches were browning on the griddle, Libra and Marina came out of the bedroom. Marina made tea and Gryphon tossed a salad while Libra and Lelindia set the table and Brendan watched the sandwiches to make sure they didn't burn.

Lunch was a lively affair, the discussion focused on the farmers market. This time he could join in the conversation. "That woodworker three stalls down was pretty impressive. Gorgeous pieces. I really liked the pair of bedside tables. Does he do anything larger?"

"Like what?" Gryphon asked.

"Dressers? Bedframes?" The bed in Libra's room was serviceable, but plain and uninspired. Only the rich colors of the bedding gave it punch. Since he planned to be spending time with her in that bed going forward, he'd prefer something with more character and style. He had no doubt Libra would be all for it. She delighted in surrounding herself with beauty.

Gryphon's look made it clear he knew exactly why Brendan was asking. "I imagine he could handle larger pieces. But they'd be pricey."

That last bit was an intentional jab, a reminder that he still hadn't told Libra about his wealth.

He gave Gryphon a subtle nod. He'd be rectifying that issue right after lunch.

As the meal wound down, Libra's emotional state ramped up, almost like she was anticipating the discussion he'd planned to have with her. As they stood to clear the dishes, he caught her elbow and lowered his voice. "Would you be up for taking a walk with me after this?"

Surprise flickered through her emotional field but was quickly overrun by anxiety. "Um, I was hoping we could go to the greenhouse."

"With Marina and Lelindia?" That would torpedo his plan.

"No, just us."

Ah. Well, that would work out fine. "Sounds good to me."

Some of her anxiety faded as she glanced down to where he still held her arm. "Me, too."

Oh, boy. He'd been so focused on talking to her, explaining his situation, that he hadn't considered how *alone* they would be. Or what could happen if he let himself get distracted. She was very distracting, especially when she looked at him the way she was now.

He dropped his hand, reining himself in. "Good."

She smiled softly, snagging his plate and hers before heading to the kitchen.

You're going to talk to her, Brendan. Just talk. No touching until you've said what you need to say.

It was good advice. And the smart thing to do. But he had doubts he'd be able to stick to it once he and Libra were closed into the warm and lush confines of the greenhouse.

Fifteen minutes later, they walked hand in hand along the path. Clouds had moved in, obscuring the sun and dropping the temperature. But he wasn't the least bit cold with Libra by his side.

He could still sense her anxiety, but there was an eagerness to her emotions, too. It reminded him of how he felt right before the first plunge of a rollercoaster.

She unlocked the door, closing it with a soft click after they'd stepped inside.

He took a steadying breath before facing her.

A goddess of the forest gazed back at him.

Yep, he'd been right. He was toast.

He pulled her into his arms without conscious thought. "I do want to talk, but–" His lips came down on hers, cutting off his own words.

She melted against him, her body aligning with his as perfectly as it had last night. Their coats provided extra bulk, which lessened the physical impact. He blocked thoughts of what could happen if they took off those coats, and instead focused on her mouth. Her delicious, tempting, sensual mouth.

The kiss lasted–minutes, hours, days–a feast he couldn't get enough of. The first time he lifted his head, her moan of protest brought him back for more. But it was the stroke of her hand across the fly of his jeans that finally drove him to break contact and put some distance between them. "We can't... go there." Talking took serious effort. Not reaching for her again took even more. "At least, not yet."

She gave herself a little shake, like she was waking from a dream. "You're right. I need to tell you something first."

"You do?" He'd thought he'd be the one doing all the talking. Maybe she wanted to share Marina's concerns about their whirlwind behavior. "Do you mind if I go first?" He wanted to put some of her fears in perspective, clear the air before they moved forward.

She hesitated, a flicker in her emotional field before she nodded. "That's fine."

"Okay." Unfastening his coat, he hung it on one of the pegs by the wall, adding hers beside it when she handed it to him.

She looked so fetching in her red sweatshirt and jeans, her color high. He wanted to kiss her again, but instead he leaned against the wash rack and crossed his arms.

She stood a couple meters away, her hands folded in front of her, waiting.

"There's something important you should know about me, something Gryphon figured out when he saw my plane. I don't allow it to define me, but it's a factor in how I live my life, and it could be a great benefit to you. Marina and Gryphon, too."

That got a reaction. Her emotional field flared with curiosity and eagerness.

"I come from a very wealthy family."

She blinked, like she'd been expecting something else.

"My ancestors founded the aerospace company I now own. My dad ran it until he died. Currently, my management team is handling day-to-day operations until I finish my doctorate. At that point, I'll be taking on a more hands-on role."

Her eagerness faded, replaced by a wariness he didn't like.

He soldiered on. "We're the largest aerospace tech provider on the planet. We have contracts with the Fleet as well as private companies, providing R&D, ship design and construction, and onsite installations from here to the Outer Rim."

Her wariness upshifted to dread. "The Outer Rim."

Not the response he wanted.

She swallowed, a tremor in her voice. "You spend a lot of time in space?"

"Not at the moment, although I will when I take over. But don't worry, we'll be able to travel together. I wouldn't leave you behind."

He'd hoped that last part would swing her back from her downward spiral, but instead her emotions screamed at him, hating every word he was saying. Clearly, he was going about this all wrong.

He plowed forward, addressing the concern he suspected was generating her anxiety. "I'm not saying you'd have to be separated from Marina and Gryphon. They can come, too."

Rather than soothing her, his reassurance propelled her toward panic. She shook her head.

Panic bit into him, too. "Don't you see? If you're with me, you won't have to be afraid. I can take you anywhere in Fleet space you want to go, introduce you to the best minds in metaphysics. No one will be able to take advantage of you. Instead of hiding, you can make the most of your gifts."

He took a step forward, but she backed away, her hands lifting like they had last night when she'd fought the drunk. He froze.

She kept shaking her head, the color draining from her face as pain lanced through her emotional field. "I can't do that."

"Do what?"

"Go. Out there!" She swung her arm in an arc toward the ceiling.

"Why not? You'll be safe. I promise."

"No."

"No?" What kind of answer was that? Especially after he'd hit on all the potential concerns he'd anticipated. "What are you afraid of?" Certainly not being hurt. After what he'd seen and been told last night, even in the vacuum of space, nothing short of a hull breach was likely to take her down.

"I can't leave Earth."

The finality in her words sliced him like blades. But he wasn't about to stop fighting. "Why not?"

Pain and terror wrestled for dominance in her emotional field. Her beautiful eyes now looked bleak, haunted. She drew a shuddering breath, then lifted her chin. "Because I'm not Human."

He heard the words. They were in Galactic English, his native tongue. But he didn't understand them. "What?"

She spoke without inflection, without emotion. "I'm. Not. Human."

Comprehension didn't trickle in. It hit like a typhoon, knocking him back against the wash rack as the room spun. Her healing ability, her energy field, her protective shield... "Not human."

And yet his mind rebelled, launching denials like arrows. "That can't be. I... We..." He'd touched her, kissed her, been *inside* her for goodness sakes. She was human. Had to be.

"It's parallel evolution. My planet is Earth-like, same star type, same gravity."

He clutched the edge of the wash rack for support. "You're an alien?"

Her nod pushed a bubble of hysteria into his throat. He choked it back down. *Well, Brendan, you always wanted to explore the galaxy and meet alien species.* He'd just never anticipated this type of first contact scenario. An intimate first contact.

For a millisecond he considered the possibility that she was lying, or that she was delusional. But he discarded the idea just as quickly. Her abilities were far beyond anything humans had achieved. If he'd been less focused on his attraction to her and more on the objective science of her abilities, he probably would have suspected her alien origins long before now.

He stared at her, the beat of his heart urging him forward while his rational mind held him back, his emotions caught in the tug-of-war. "Why didn't you tell me?"

She flinched. "It didn't matter if you knew until..." She hesitated, trepidation in her eyes and emotional field. "Until we were going to be mates."

Were. Past tense. His heart registered the change and whimpered. "You don't want to mate with me anymore?" The term itself should have been a clue. Marriage had been a foreign concept to her. An *alien* concept. She'd always said mate.

She shifted her weight but didn't look away. "I've never wanted anything more."

The desperate longing in her emotional field got him moving. Pushing away from the rack he crossed to her, halting within touching distance.

Her emotions were as turbulent as his, but she didn't move a muscle.

Reaching out, he captured her hand, holding it up between them. Same bone structure, same skin, same warmth. "You look human."

"You look Suulh."

The defiance in her statement brought his gaze to her face. She was watching him very carefully. "Suulh?" The word was different too, the vowel sounds longer, giving it a lyrical quality. Just like her accent. Did her entire language sound like that? "That's the name of your race?"

The haunted look returned to her eyes. "Yes."

Pieces started moving, snippets from previous conversations taking on new meaning. "You weren't born on Earth, were you? You came here after your parents died."

The heavy pulse of her emotions and the moisture that coated her eyes gave him his answer. "Yes."

"Why Earth?"

She looked away, her gaze on something he couldn't see. "We could be safe here."

Safe. Everything she said and did always circled back to that. "You weren't safe on your homeworld?"

A shudder passed through her petite frame, her shoulders drawing in. "No."

His protective instincts overrode every other consideration. Tugging on her hand, he pulled her into his arms.

She stiffened for a moment, but as he used his palm to make slow circles on her back, her cheek pressed into his chest, her body softening against his.

It felt so right. So perfect. Human, alien, Suulh. Did it really matter? He'd told her he didn't let his wealth define him. He'd be a hypocrite if he allowed her biology to define her. "I'm sorry, Libra."

She sighed, snuggling closer as he continued his soothing caress. "Me, too."

His heartbeat calmed, his muscles relaxing as he focused on the here and now. She'd hit him with a punch he hadn't expected, but she was still Libra. Still the woman he loved. All the wonderful, amazing qualities she possessed hadn't changed, only his perspective of them. And that was only a problem if he allowed it to be.

"You don't mind that I'm an alien?" she asked.

He smiled. Maybe she could read his mind. He lobbed the question back at her. "You don't mind that I'm an alien?"

She gave a little snuffle snort, tilting her head back to meet his gaze. "No."

"Neither do I."

She was extraordinary, everything he'd ever dreamed of. Now he had a clearer understanding of why. That knowledge was causing him to reevaluate his assumptions, but the longer he gazed into her eyes, the more certain he became that he didn't want to alter any of his conclusions. He wanted her with him, always.

Thirty-Two

Libra watched the interplay of thoughts and emotions on Brendan's handsome face. He'd been shocked by her revelation, but he'd handled it well, considering. And the way he was looking at her now filled her with hope.

Which left one dangling question. "Then you'll stay?"

He frowned. "Stay?"

"With me. Here."

His gentle caress stopped. "You mean permanently?"

She nodded, but a trickle of anxiety dripped down her neck at the look in his eyes.

"I can't stay here permanently."

The trickle turned into a steady stream. "Why not?"

"Why not?" He released her, stepping back. "I told you. I own a company that operates throughout Fleet space. My family's company. I'm needed there. I can't stay."

The anxiety changed from liquid to solid, clamping on with iron tentacles.

His expression softened. "But you can come with me. No one needs to know you're Suulh. Not unless you choose to tell them. I'll protect your secret. Protect you."

He still didn't understand. "You can't."

"What do you mean?"

The tentacles squeezed. She started pacing, fighting their grip. "Marina and I are being hunted."

"Hunted?"

"The race that destroyed our homeworld wants our abilities. To make us their slaves." She glanced at him. He looked too stunned to speak, so she continued. "They are heartless, cruel, manipulative beings who ravage everything in their path. If Gryphon hadn't stolen one of their ships, and he and Marina hadn't been able to smuggle me off our planet, I would have…" Her throat closed up as the nightmarish memories assaulted her.

She placed a hand on her stomach and engaged her energy field, struggling to maintain her composure. Its touch soothed her, pushing back the horror. "We fled, always on the run, never knowing if or when they would catch us. And then we encountered our first Humans. We couldn't believe how similar they were to us. They accepted us as Human. That was the first time we had hope."

And then she'd seen Gaia, the first Human colony, which looked so much like Feylahn. She'd cried for an hour that day as Marina had held her. "We tried living on Gaia for a while, but we never felt safe there. The planet had no defenses, and the Humans there were mostly peaceful farmers. They wouldn't have been any help if we'd been discovered. So we came here, to Earth."

She turned to face him. His muscles were tensed like he was preparing for battle. "Here, we could disappear into a sea of billions, secure behind the planet's defense systems. We'd found our refuge, our haven. For the first time, we could build a life, a real life, without always looking over our shoulders." She held his gaze, pleading for understanding. "As long as we stayed hidden."

His jaw worked. "Are you talking about Setarips? Are they the ones who destroyed your world?"

She shook her head. "No." She'd heard stories of the reptilian aliens who attacked Human settlements and outposts. "We never encountered them."

"So, this is a race the Fleet has never come across?"

She nodded.

His gaze softened, his posture relaxing a bit. "Doesn't that indicate they've stopped hunting you? How long has it been since you left?"

"Thirteen Earth years."

He stepped forward. "That's a long time, Libra. They've probably given up by now."

"Maybe they have." She'd entertained the possibility before, although she didn't believe it. "But I'm not willing to bet Marina and Lelindia's lives on it. Or my daughter's."

Brendan blew out a breath, shoving his hands through his hair. "So, you're going to hide out here for the rest of your life? Never leave?" He didn't sound angry. He sounded indescribably sad.

"Yes."

He turned away, his shoulders hunching. "Is that the life you want for Lelindia? For our daughter?"

Pain flared in her chest. "I want them to be safe."

He turned back. "Safety is relative. And eventually Lelindia's going to make her own choices. So would our daughter. What will you do if they want to leave?"

Panic set in, anger chasing right behind it. "They wouldn't. They'll understand the risks. The need to stay together."

"And what about me?" He took a step closer, then another. "I'm a pilot, Libra. An explorer. My company has been in my family for generations. We've all traveled to the stars, expanded the boundaries of discovery. Would you want me to stay hidden away here for the rest of my life, too?"

"You could study our energy abilities. You said you wanted to."

"I did." His gaze searched hers. For what, she couldn't say. "But you're asking me to give up everything. My home, my company, my dreams. All because of a fear that may be unfounded."

Her memories of Feylahn, their mad flight to escape, rammed to the front again, the terrifying images ripping at her from the inside out. "If you really understood, you wouldn't say that."

He sighed, his gaze dropping to the floor. "Maybe you're right. I can't imagine what you've been through." When he looked up, the pain in his eyes knocked the air from her lungs. "But I can't give up everything to live in fear. Even to be with you."

She opened her mouth, but no words came out.

He leaned down, his lips brushing hers in a whisper of a kiss. "I will always love you."

Stepping back, he grabbed his coat off the hook, pulled it on, and left the greenhouse, the door clicking shut behind him.

Thirty-Three

"Train should be here in ten minutes."

Brendan stared out the window of Gryphon's vehicle. The puddles on the station parking lot reflected the clouds above. The rain had started to fall after he'd left the greenhouse and hadn't stopped. It seemed fitting, matching his mood and the outlook for his immediate future.

He'd planned to call a transport to take him to the station, but Gryphon had insisted on driving him instead. He'd been too emotionally exhausted to argue.

Libra hadn't returned to the cabin while he'd packed his bag. Probably for the best. He wanted to remember her standing amid the lush greenery she loved so well, even if that image burned white-hot in his mind.

He turned to Gryphon. "Just so you know, she told me about the Suulh. The attack. Why you're hiding here."

Gryphon's eyes didn't give anything away. "I figured she had. Is that why you're leaving? Because you can't accept her for who she is?"

Indignation heated his voice. "Of course I can. I don't care if she's human, Suulh, or some other species I've never met. I love her."

For better or worse, which was looking a whole lot worse. "I love her more than I ever imagined I could love anyone. Leaving her… it's killing me. But she's determined to remain isolated here for the rest of her life. She won't even consider expanding the confines of her safety bubble. And she's planning to put those same restrictions on Lelindia and our daughter—her daughter—if she can." He forced himself to make the mental amendment. Libra would probably still have a daughter, but the child wouldn't be his. If the thought made him want to swear a blue streak at the universe, well, so be it.

Gryphon's hands tightened on the wheel. "She said that?"

"Yes. I know it's her fear talking, but that doesn't change the facts. She says she wants a life with me, but only within the narrow boundaries she's set for us, one that fits in her current paradigm. I'm the one who'd have to forfeit everything to be with her."

"And you're not willing to do that?"

"No. She wants to hold onto her fear like a shield, allow it to control our lives. I can't live like that."

"What if you can change her mind?"

Brendan blinked. He hadn't expected Gryphon to advocate for him.

"Shocked you into silence, boy?"

"Uh, yeah."

Gryphon turned in his seat to face him. "I've known Libra since she was younger than Lelindia. She was so different then. Always smiling and laughing. Full of mischief and a childlike bravado."

A tiny smile creased his cheek, fading as quickly as it appeared. "But then it all came apart."

Brendan kept silent, waiting.

"She hasn't smiled or laughed like that in a long time." He shot Brendan a look. "Until you dropped out of the sky."

That warmed him. "I love making her laugh." It had become his raison d'etre from the first moment he'd seen her smile.

"I know." Gryphon tapped out a beat on the steering wheel with his thumb, like an accompaniment to his thoughts. "I love Libra like a sister. Or a daughter. But she's as stubborn as they come. Always has been."

He'd already run afoul of that particular trait.

"I hadn't realized how much she's been living in the shadows until you came into her life. You lit something in her that I thought was extinguished forever. And I would hate to see that light go out."

So would he, even if he wouldn't be there to see it. "What makes you think I can change her mind?"

"Because you're an optimist. And damn good at reading her. But more important, she's bonded to you. Since you're not Suulh, you may not understand what that means, but it's a powerful force in our lives. I have that connection with Marina. I would fly through a supernova for that woman."

Gryphon's throat worked in a convulsive swallow as his gaze shifted to the forest in the distance. "I can't imagine my life without her. And she would give her last breath to heal me." He looked back at Brendan. "Libra's no different. And from what I've seen, neither are you."

No, he wasn't. He'd told Libra the truth. No matter what happened, he would love her for the rest of his life.

"There are some things about herself, about her past, she may never reveal." He grimaced. "You'd have to accept that going in."

"I could live with that. But what about my company? I can't run it while living like a hermit here."

Gryphon shrugged. "Who's watching things right now?"

"My management team."

"Any reason they can't keep doing it?"

"For how long?"

"That depends on you. Is it worth risking the safety of your family so you can lead the life you envisioned for yourself?"

That was a tougher question.

Gryphon's mouth tightened. "Let me put it to you this way. I love to fly. I recognized your plane because I study anything I can get my hands on having to do with flying."

"I figured." His questions and observations had been very on point.

"Did Libra tell you I piloted the starship that got us off Feylahn?"

He nodded.

"Before we had to flee, I had visions of exploring the galaxy, charting new systems. But I haven't flown since we arrived on Earth, since Marina and I mated. That was a choice I was willing to make to protect my family. And I've never regretted that sacrifice for one second. My mate and my daughter are worth it."

And here he'd thought Gryphon was living his dream, tucked away in the cozy cabin.

"I'm not saying you'd have to give up everything. Maybe not even your company. Libra needs to grow, too, to get past her fears and embrace life. I believe you can help her do that. And being with her will change you in ways you can't imagine. To be loved by a Sahzade or Nedale is a rare gift, if you're brave enough to accept it."

"Sahzade and Nedale?" Lelindia had called Libra Sahzade when they were in the greenhouse. Libra had claimed it was a nickname.

Gryphon quirked a brow. "I see she didn't explain that. The Nedale is the healer of the Suulh race. That's Marina. The Sahzade is the guardian, the leader. That's Libra."

"Leader?" His mind stumbled over the word, throwing him off balance. "Are you telling me Libra's the leader of the entire Suulh race?"

"She was supposed to be. And still is, for the few of us who are left. It's one of the reasons she's so strong-willed. It's her job to make decisions that will protect our people from harm."

He stared at Gryphon. *Stellar light.* And here he'd worried Libra might be intimidated by the power he wielded through his company. He didn't know what real power was until he met her. "That explains why she's so determined to keep you all safe, no matter the cost."

Gryphon nodded. "It's in her blood. If she hadn't been so young, and in a state of shock when we smuggled her off Feylahn, she would have fought to stay and defend the city. And we would have lost her forever."

Gryphon's emotional pain dug into Brendan's gut, reminding him how close he'd come to never knowing Libra at all.

A whistle blew, announcing the arrival of the monorail.

Gryphon glanced at the platform, then back at Brendan. "Time's up, boy. What's it going to be? Take that train back to the path you were on before you crashed into Libra? Or stay here and see where the path you're forging together will lead?"

The weight of the decision pressed down on him, making him sweat. And he had about two minutes to choose.

If he got on the train, he knew exactly where it would take him. He also had a pretty clear image of what his future would look like.

If he stayed, he'd be venturing into the unknown with no guarantees. He might never be the head of his company, might never live in the family home in Hawaii, even if Libra worked through her fears and decided to expand her world into his.

And he certainly couldn't pressure her. That would be unfair. If he did this, he couldn't have a hidden agenda. He'd need to be completely focused on being together, creating a family, living a life of their making, whatever that looked like.

His parents had wanted that for him, had encouraged him to forge his own future. They'd never assumed he would take over the company. That had been his choice. And they'd never imposed their ideas about what he should or shouldn't become. All they'd ever asked of him was that he would follow his heart, be true to himself.

Their love for him and each other had always been his guiding star. He needed to trust it to guide him now.

"I'm staying."

Thirty-Four

The rain pattered the hood of Libra's sweatshirt as she followed the path toward the fallen redwood, but she didn't care enough to summon her shield.

The darkening grey gloom told her the sun was setting behind the clouds, the night closing in.

She didn't care about that, either.

Brendan had left. She'd felt it keenly, her ability to track him telling her exactly when he'd headed for town. The pain that had lanced through her heart had almost dropped her to the floor.

So she'd pulled into herself and shut out the world. Shut out her emotions, shut out her senses, shut out everything. The void was the only safe place for her now.

Her shoes made squishing noises as she trudged through the gathering mud puddles. Ordinarily she delighted in the rain—the invigorating scent, the glistening droplets, the patter on the leaves and ground. But delight wasn't an emotion she expected to feel any time soon.

How had it all gone so wrong? She'd been certain she and Brendan would spend the rest of their lives together. That he would be the father of the next Sahzade. Now that dream fell like ash at her feet.

Before they'd touched, before he'd stoked her desire, the concept of a daughter had been a vague shadow seen out of the corner of her eye, ephemeral and distant. Try as she might, she'd never been able to work up any enthusiasm for a physical relationship with Wolf. Sex with him would have been perfunctory, necessary to carry on the Sahzade line.

But Brendan inspired her, igniting her passion and lighting up her senses. Gazing into his eyes as they'd joined had brought her future into sharp focus, giving her daughter a form and presence that filled her with joy.

And trapping her in a prison she couldn't escape.

Now her future lay in fractured shards like a shattered mirror, her daughter's image a jagged scar.

Wolf would still agree to mate with her. He was devoted to her, and to continuing the Sahzade line. But the experience of conceiving a child with him would rip out what was left of her heart.

Her only hope was that her daughter would be able to pull the pieces back together. Wolf would never awaken her energy field, and no Human she encountered would, either. She knew that with absolute certainty. Brendan was extraordinary.

A blessing, and a curse.

But she couldn't be with him. His life was out amongst the stars. Hers was here. She'd tried to convince him to stay—an act of cowardly desperation—but thankfully he'd been strong enough to do what had to be done.

He was too full of light to live in the shadows of her existence. She just hadn't wanted to accept it.

A raindrop struck her cheek, startling her. She swiped it away, a burst of anger at her selfishness making the movement jerky.

Brendan deserved so much more than she had to give. He'd tried to share his light with her, and for a brief moment, her world had glowed like a sunbeam. But rather than embracing that warmth, she'd tried to dim it, tried to draw him into her cave. What had she been thinking?

Her boot caught on a rock and she stumbled, her shield flaring as her shoulder clipped a nearby tree trunk. She shoved away from it, stalking down the path as her anger built.

How could she have been so blind? Had she honestly expected Brendan to move into their small cabin and cut all ties with the outside world? To give up everything for her? He wasn't a Suulh. He didn't know she was the Sahzade, the most sought-after member of her race. And even if he did, he wouldn't care. He wanted her for who she was, not for her lineage or what she could do.

But she'd responded to his generous heart and empathy with fear and demands, driving him away.

The dark shape of the fallen redwood loomed ahead, the fading daylight barely outlining the tunnel underneath. She halted beneath its sheltering bulk, staring at the spot where Brendan had first awoken a fire that still burned.

She had a connection with him that defied description, deeper and stronger than anything she'd imagined possible. The power of their bonding had transcended Human and Suulh, proving he was the mate of her heart and soul.

Proving he was *her* mate.

She sucked in a breath, her body swaying as the truth hit her like an energy blast. Memories of their joining flooded her mind, making her tremble. She reached out a shaky hand, touching the ancient redwood. As its energy blended with hers, its wisdom and understanding plumbed the depths of her being.

She'd experienced the essence of what it meant to be Suulh with a HUMAN. How had she not understood how rare and precious that gift was? Why had she not fought to find a solution, rather than throwing up shields?

She knew why. Because she'd allowed her fear to eclipse her joy.

And now Brendan was on a train, leaving her forever.

A giant fist encircled her chest, squeezing the air from her lungs.

She had to stop him. Had to find him before he was too far away for her to reach.

Whirling around, she raced up the shadowy path, her shield knocking aside anything that got in the way of her mad sprint.

He couldn't be far. She'd get Gryphon to drive her to the next station. Or the one after that. How fast did the train travel?

Air shot in and out of her lungs as she whipped past tree after tree and leapt over a rocky outcropping. Reaching out with her senses, she swept the area for Brendan's unique resonance. And almost collided with a massive trunk when she pinpointed him less than a kilometer away.

He'd come back!

Her shriek startled several birds roosting in the branches. Before they'd reached open air she was running again, her hood falling back as a surge of emotion gave her feet wings. She drove forward as she sensed Brendan drawing closer.

"Brendan!" she bellowed like a foghorn in the gloom.

"Libra!"

The sweetest sound she'd ever heard.

Laughter bubbled up as she made a beeline for him, leaving the clear ground of the path and cutting through the trees. He must have seen her shield, or heard the ruckus she was making, because he was facing her as she tore down a small hill beside the creek to where he waited.

She barely slowed as she flew into his open arms, knocking him back against the nearest tree. "I'm so sorry." She peppered his throat with kisses, the only part of him she could reach with his arms locking her against his chest. "I'm so, so sorry. Please don't go."

His grip eased enough that he could pull back to meet her gaze. "I'm not going anywhere." Then his lips came down on hers.

That first touch made her whimper, tears pushing against her closed eyelids as she drank in the taste of him. Her energy field surrounded them, creating a warm cocoon with Brendan at the heart.

He inhaled sharply, breaking off the kiss and pressing her more tightly against his muscled body. "I couldn't do it. I couldn't leave. This is worth fighting for."

"Yes, it is." She brushed her lips against his before pulling back to gaze into his eyes. "I was running after you."

"You were?"

"Uh-huh. I thought maybe Gryphon and I could catch you at the next station. Then I sensed you here and... kinda lost my mind."

"I know the feeling." He kissed her again, this time more tenderly. When he lifted his head, his face was luminous. "The thought of never seeing you again, never holding you." He shook his head. "I don't want that future. I want to be with you, whatever that looks like."

She had at least one piece of that puzzle to offer. "I think it looks like our daughter."

Heat flared in his eyes. "I like the sound of that."

She liked everything about this moment. But she needed to know one thing. "What about your company?"

His gaze grew solemn. "I don't have a long-term solution, but Gryphon reminded me that my management team can handle it for now. That buys us time. We'll figure it out. Together. And in the meantime." The heat returned to his eyes, his grip on her hips tightening, pressing her against the swell in his jeans. "We can get started on the next Sahzade."

She jerked in surprise. "Gryphon told you?"

"That you're the leader of the Suulh? And that Marina's the race's healer? Yes. Which I assume means Lelindia is, too. You can fill in the details later, but I understand how important that relationship is to both of you. I can't wait to watch our daughter and Lelindia grow up together. And I hope our little Sahzade will be every bit as caring and protective as her mother."

His words filled her with a warmth that didn't have anything to do with her energy field. "And I hope she'll be every bit as optimistic and empathic as her father." She couldn't imagine a better guide than Brendan to light her daughter's way through the uncertain future.

His smile shone like a beacon, drawing her lips to his. "The best of you, and the best of me. Sounds like the perfect combination."

As his lips touched hers, triggering a wave of heat and light, she couldn't imagine anything she'd love more.

Epilogue

When Libra had told Brendan she wanted a Suulh mating ceremony rather than a wedding, he'd agreed without question. She'd also set the date for midday on the spring equinox.

The sooner the better, as far as he was concerned. Suulh tradition didn't allow them to conceive the next Sahzade until after the ceremony was complete.

Not that he was complaining. They'd been getting in a lot of practice in the last two months, and the results had been outstanding.

But now the moment had finally arrived. He tugged on the sleeve of his flowing jacket, a gift from the six Suulh who had arrived from Gaia to attend the ceremony. He still didn't have the full story from Libra on how the nine of them had made their escape from Feylahn, or why the six had chosen to remain on Gaia—the work to help her process her pain was a marathon, not a sprint—but he knew enough to thank the stars for the group gathered around him.

The three men stood in a semicircle behind him and Gryphon, their backs to the ancient redwood as it bore silent witness to the beauty and wonder of this day. A misty rain during the night had enriched the colors and scents around them, the sparkle of sunbeams on the droplets creating prisms of light.

But Brendan's gaze was fixed on the path that led back to the cabin. Libra would be walking down that path with the rest of the women soon, and he didn't want to miss a millisecond.

Gryphon rested a hand on his shoulder. "You look ready to levitate, boy."

Pretty accurate. Right now he felt like he could fly. "I've waited my whole life for this."

Gryphon's knowing chuckle made him glance over. "I know exactly what you mean."

An understanding passed between them deeper than words. Gryphon was the one person who truly knew what this day meant to him. On that bleak afternoon two months ago, sitting in the rain-soaked parking lot at the train station, Gryphon had told him being loved by a Nedale or Sahzade was an amazing gift. Truer words had never been spoken.

Yesterday he'd given Libra a gift in return. He'd taken her out to the site that, after construction was completed, would be their new home.

The five of them had been getting along fine in the cabin, but the space simply wasn't big enough for the expanse of their future plans. Besides, the more he learned about the Suulh, the more he wanted a home that reflected their culture, and the unique relationship between the Sahzade and Nedale.

Gryphon had drawn up rough sketches of the house Libra and Marina had lived in on Feylahn, which resembled a geodesic dome with half-moon wings, one for each family. Learning that the two families had shared the same home for countless generations reinforced his desire to create a similar nurturing space for his new family.

His only concern as he'd driven Libra to the property was that her fear would make her reject the visual representation of the Suulh culture. The forest site wasn't visible from the road, and he and Gryphon had scaled down the original design and planned adaptations that would help the house blend in with other structures in the area, but those rational arguments wouldn't necessarily hold sway.

Except they had. Libra's response had been everything he'd hoped for and more. Rather than fear, she'd surrounded him with joy and love, kissing him senseless.

That same exuberant joy flowed over him now, not from within, but through his empathic senses. He turned his attention to the path.

Libra was near.

He spotted Lelindia first, leading the procession, her emerald green energy field as vibrant as the lush greenery around them. Her dark hair swayed with each measured and methodical step, her head held high, showing a maturity that belied her age. No skipping today, although she still radiated energy like a firefly.

However, it was the angel behind her that stole the breath from his lungs. Libra's pearlescent energy field flowed around the curves of her body, highlighting the form-fitting drape of white material that emphasized her generous bust, narrow waist, and hips before separating into a rainbow of color strips interwoven with white that fell in graceful layers, fluttering and dancing with each step.

Marina walked behind her, her emerald green energy field making the pearlescent glow appear even more radiant.

Something bumped his shoulder.

"Breathe," Gryphon murmured in an undertone.

He inhaled, air pouring into his lungs, the lightheadedness that had been creeping over him fading. His gaze locked with Libra's, their connection grounding him. This goddess of the forest was his mate. His future. His love. And he was hers.

Her energy field flared as she held his gaze, the look in her eyes making his heart pound.

The procession drew closer, the other three Suulh women following behind Marina, the varied colors of their energy fields creating a rippling rainbow.

He felt the brush of Gryphon's energy field against his side as it engaged, sensed Gryphon's strength coming through the vibrant yellow-gold, the joy in his heart as they watched Lelindia, Libra, and Marina approach.

Their family.

The past two months had taught him a lot about the depth of the interconnection of the Sahzade and Nedale lines, his empathic senses allowing him to delve into the essence of what it meant to be a part of that bond, to be Suulh. Their acceptance of him as one of their own humbled him, as did their generosity of spirit.

Hopefully one day Mary Kay would meet them. He'd debated inviting her to the ceremony, but he wasn't ready to tell her the truth, and he didn't want to lie. For now, it was enough that she knew he was happy, and that his future plans were changing. She'd already begun preparing the management team for a more long-term role with the company. Maybe after the house was built, he could fly her out for a housewarming gathering.

His gaze moved to Lelindia as she stopped in front of them, her usually laughing brown eyes solemn. Libra and Marina stopped as well, Libra stepping slightly to her left, Marina slightly to her right, so they formed a V with Lelindia at the point.

Lelindia gazed at her father first, then turned her focus to him. When she spoke, it was in the Suulh language, but he was able to understand the meaning thanks to Marina's language coaching.

"I am Lelindia, daughter of Marina, Nedale of the Suulh." The words flowed with the grace and beauty of music. He knew the hours she'd put into practicing to get it right. "The Sahzade Libra has chosen her mate, the Human Brendan, as the father-to-be of my energy sister."

Energy sister. Today he would become Libra's mate, but their decision would impact the Suulh race for all time. He'd known that intellectually, but Lelindia's uncharacteristically steady gaze drove the point home.

"Do you accept this gift given freely by the Sahzade?"

His gaze rose to Libra. She was still too far away to touch, but her energy field reached out to him, the gentle caress making his breath hitch. "With all my heart."

A giggle made him glance down.

Lelindia grinned up at him, her natural enthusiasm chasing away the serious overtones now that her job was done. Grabbing his hand in hers, she turned to face Libra and Marina, taking her dad's hand on the other side to form a three-person chain.

A smile flitted over Libra's face before she pivoted toward Marina.

Marina held out her hands, palms up. Libra clasped them in hers, her energy field and Marina's flowing toward each other through the connection, weaving in and out to form a stunning tapestry of rich green and pearlescent white.

A telltale shimmer coated Marina's eyes as she gazed at Libra. "I am Marina, daughter of Breaa, Nedale of the Suulh." Her voice hitched, her emotions far from the calm sea he was used to sensing from her.

Libra was fighting a similar battle.

So was he.

Marina pushed on. "Libra, Sahzade of the Suulh and my energy sister, you have chosen your mate, and he has accepted your gift." She paused, glancing at him with a watery smile.

He could feel the soul-deep happiness washing over her, the joy she felt for Libra, and him. The hope for their future together.

He projected his own feelings at her, chief among them gratitude for all the love and support she'd given them along their journey to this day. If she hadn't been in his corner from day one, he probably wouldn't be here.

She gave a subtle nod, acknowledging the non-verbal thank you. Focusing on Libra, she took a long, slow breath. "This bonding is a gift to all Suulh. Nedale and Sahzade, throughout the ages, have nurtured and protected our people." Her emotions surged like a cresting wave, contorting her face as she struggled to maintain her composure. She cleared her throat, but it did little to remove the huskiness from her voice. "Now we await the conception of the Sahzade-to-be, Lelindia's energy sister, to complete the circle again, as your birth—" Her voice broke on the last word, tears spilling down her cheeks. "Completed mine."

Droplets of moisture tracked down his face as their emotions, and those of everyone gathered around them, washed over him.

Libra stepped forward and enveloped Marina in a hug.

He'd been in emotionally charged situations before, but nothing like this. The interconnection of the Suulh, their inherent empathy for each other, felt completely different from the dissonance that was standard in a gathering of humans. Here, in this place of beauty and light, harmony reigned. Love and joy wrapped around him, tinged with the aching sadness for all the Suulh had lost.

Libra turned, meeting his gaze.

And all we've found.

The words were hers. As their connection grew, he'd started picking up on her thought projections during moments of intense emotion. This certainly qualified.

She released Marina, their matching smiles filling his heart. Marina moved toward Gryphon, taking his hand, while Libra walked toward him.

Breathing got a lot harder. As did controlling the urge to reach for her. Her hair looked like spun gold as it caught the morning light, her face luminous. His angel. But it was the touch of her energy field as she took his hand that almost tumbled him over the edge.

He couldn't look away, only vaguely aware that the other six Suulh had moved to face them, completing the circle as they joined hands.

Libra squeezed his hand before her gaze swept the circle. "I am Libra, daughter of Sooree, Sahzade of the Suulh. In the name of my mother and my daughter-to-be, I pledge myself to Brendan, my mate, and to all the Suulh, past, present, and future."

Unlike Marina, her voice was strong and clear. The voice of a leader. The Sahzade of the Suulh.

Her strength and power stunned him. She had crossed time and space to reach him, risked dangers he was only beginning to comprehend. And here she stood, with the responsibility of an entire race on her shoulders, claiming him, a human, as her mate.

The reality knocked all thoughts from his head. It took him a moment to realize why she and the rest of the circle were gazing at him expectantly.

He reigned in his emotions, determined to be worthy of the incredible woman by his side. Thank goodness he'd practiced his lines as much as Lelindia. "I am Brendan, son of Emma, mate of the Sahzade." Stellar light, he loved saying that! But the critical part came next. As the Sahzade's mate, he was responsible for announcing the name he and Libra had selected for their daughter.

"I pledge to my mate, and to all Suulh, a daughter, the Sahzade-to-be, whose name shall be... Aurora."

A collective sigh went up from the Suulh, followed by an excited giggle from Lelindia. "Aurora!" she shouted, her energy field flowing out to envelop him and Gryphon in its cooling, joyous embrace.

"Aurora!" Gryphon echoed, his energy field blending with Lelindia's and flowing out to Brendan and Marina.

"Aurora!" Marina grinned at her mate, her energy field joining the chain.

The pattern continued around the circle, the energy fields of the Suulh weaving together until only Libra was untouched by their glow.

She turned her head, holding his gaze as she spoke. "Aurora. Our daughter, the future Sahzade." Her energy field flared brighter than the rest, racing around the circle like lightning, threading through the rest of the colors, binding them together in a glorious whole.

"Our daughter," he repeated, for her ears only.

Her answering smile lit him up almost as much as her energy field. "Our daughter." And judging by the warmth in her eyes and the joy in her heart, she was as eager to conceive their daughter as he was.

Aurora. Their little Sahzade. He couldn't wait to meet her.

Captain's Log

Welcome to the Starhawke Universe!

If this is your first journey into the Starhawke Universe, you may be wondering how exactly this book fits in with the rest of my series.

Guardian Mate is the origin story that precedes the beginning of my main series, Starhawke Rising. Libra and Brendan's daughter, Aurora Hawke, is the main character in that series, now an adult and captain of her own ship, the *Starhawke.* She's the core of my universe, the first character I created, and the link that ties all the other books together. If you enjoyed this story, you'll probably enjoy her series too, beginning with book one, THE DARK OF LIGHT. While romance isn't the focus of her series, is a very strong element in everything I write, which is part of the reason this book came into existence!

Romancing the Starhawke

This is the first official romance story in the Starhawke Universe. Perhaps it was inevitable that one day I'd write it. I'm the daughter of a well-known romance writer, after all. It's in my blood.

The genesis for this book was a simple concept I came up with when I first created my main character, Aurora Hawke. Because

I wanted her to have abilities beyond the scope of human experience, I gave her an alien mother and a human father. At the time, I didn't ask myself why that had occurred. Or how. I simply took it as a fact of her backstory and moved on.

However, as the Starhawke Rising series progressed, I discovered that I needed to know those answers in order to tell Aurora's story. Delving into her past and the relationship between her parents convinced me I wanted to tell their story, too.

Figuring out the path that brought Brendan and Libra together took some mental gymnastics, because I needed to stay within the framework I'd already set in the main series. Creative planning, and some very appreciated input from a dear friend who's a pilot, helped me formulate their accidental meeting. From there the characters took over, telling me their story like I was watching a private movie screening.

Fun fact – the scene between Brendan and Gryphon at the train station was one of the first scenes I wrote. For reasons that only my subconscious understands, that scene popped into my head nearly a year before I dove into the heart of the story, playing out while I was painting a wall in my house. Since I've learned to trust those flashes of inspiration, I quickly wrote out the scene and hung onto it for future reference, fully expecting that by the time the book was written, I'd have to throw out most of it. But I didn't. The finished version is more expanded than the original, but most of what I wrote that day is still there. I love it when that happens!

The character who completely captured my heart in this book, and surprised me at every turn, is Lelindia. If you've read Aurora's series, you know that as an adult she goes by the name "Mya" instead, a nickname Aurora gave her as a child. Leaping back before Aurora's birth gave me an opportunity to learn a lot more about her, to find out what kind of kid she was when her life was less complicated. Many of the answers were hinted at in her adult behavior—the way she greets her mother after they've been apart, her passion for the *Starhawke*'s greenhouse, her devotion to Aurora—but I had a great time playing cards with her in her childhood room and watching her skip around the farmers market, unburdened by the hardships that weighed her down later on. I suspect some of her natural enthusiasm will be showing itself onboard the *Starhawke* going forward.

Enjoy the journey!
Audrey

P.S. - I always write to music, and I select a different piece of music for each story, one that feeds the mood I need to get the words flowing. If you'd like to experience this story the way I did, listen to the soundtrack for *Star Trek: Insurrection* while you read.

Audrey Sharpe grew up believing in the Force and dreaming of becoming captain of the Enterprise. She's still working out the logistics of moving objects with her mind, but writing science fiction provides a pretty good alternative. When she's not off exploring the galaxy with Aurora and her crew, she lives in the Sonoran Desert, where she has an excellent view of the stars.

For more information about Audrey and the Starhawke Universe, visit her website and join the crew!

AUDREYSHARPE.COM